Till the Leaves Change

Till the Leaves Change

ERIN FLANAGAN

AN AVON CAMELOT BOOK

TILL THE LEAVES CHANGE is an original publication of Avon Books. This work has never before appeared in book form.

AVON BOOKS
A division of
The Hearst Corporation
1350 Avenue of the Americas
New York, New York 10019

Copyright © 1996 by Erin Flanagan
Published by arrangement with the author
Library of Congress Catalog Card Number: 96-96034
ISBN: 0-380-77850-5
RL: 4.5

First Avon Camelot Printing: August 1996

CAMELOT TRADEMARK REG. U.S. PAT. OFF. AND IN OTHER COUNTRIES, MARCA REGISTRADA, HECHO EN U.S.A.

Printed in the U.S.A.

OPM 10 9 8 7 6 5 4 3 2 1

*In memory of my mother
and for my other mother,
Mamalou Kassem*

CHAPTER
1

"Brouhaha."

"Who ha ha?" asked Anne.

"You sound just like a chimp," Becky said with a giggle.

I sat on my front porch swing with my oldest best friend, Becky Britton. And my newest best friend, Anne Elizabeth Clarke, of Oxford, England.

"Brouhaha," I repeated. "It's my vocabulary word for the day. It means a big fuss, an uproar."

"Sounds like my mother last night," said Becky. "All I did was ask if I could get contacts, and she brouhaha'ed all over the living room." She stood up, put one hand on her hip and did an excellent imitation of her mom. "Rebecca Britton! Contacts at the age of thirteen and a half? You've got to be kidding! I can't even get you to look after the cat. Why on earth would I buy you something so expensive and easy to lose?"

Anne and I laughed. Becky bowed and took her seat on the swing.

"Sounds a bit like my mum, too," said Anne. "I asked to get my hair permed, and she accused me of turning into a spoiled American teenager!"

"Oh, well, that part is true," I said.

Anne looked sideways at me, not sure whether to laugh or slug me. "You're pulling my leg again, isn't it?"

I laughed. "You English are so serious!"

"Well, are all Americans so utterly obsessed with their vocabularies?" she asked with a smile.

Becky poked me in my skinny rib cage. "This American right here is obsessed *and* smart. Are you still going to take that test to see if you can skip ninth grade, Louise?"

I carefully filed the "brouhaha" card back into the box of vocabulary words and set it on the porch. "Well, I haven't really decided, but I think maybe I will. That's why I'm sitting here studying instead of enjoying the first day of summer vacation, like everyone else in this town."

"Well, I hope you don't take the stupid test, and if you do take it, I hope you don't pass it!" said Becky. "Not to be mean or jealous, or anything. I just don't want you to go off to high school without me!"

I knew what she meant. We'd been friends since second grade; which is forever in this university town where people are always moving in and out.

"Well," said Anne, "I, for one, think it'll be smashing if you make it; a real honor!"

"That's because you're moving back to England at the end of this summer, so it's no biggy to you!" wailed Becky. "I'll end up losing both of you, and it stinks!"

I patted her back. I was good at calming Becky down; I'd had lots and lots of practice. "Come on, Beck, you should be used to it by now. You know this place—people always coming and going."

"The coming is fine, it's the going I hate!" she said.

"Going? My God! Look at the time! Mum will have my head on a silver tray if I miss her precious tea time again!" Anne sprang from the swing and flew down the path, her long, flaxen hair bouncing behind her. She turned and waved. " 'Bye, y'all!" she said, deftly imitating our Virginia drawl.

We laughed and waved back.

"So—do you really want to skip a grade and go to high school, Louise? Really?" asked Becky.

I leaned back and watched a cardinal swoop into view and land on the bird feeder. "Oh, I dunno. Kind of yes, and kind of no."

"How decisive of you."

"Well, it's hard to decide, Beck! I want to, because then school won't be so deathly boring for me. Mom thinks I should at least take the test, and my stepdad thinks I should . . ."

"Well, your best friend thinks you shouldn't."

"I know. I don't want to leave you and all our

friends, either." I shuddered as I thought of something even worse: undressing during gym class. "And I don't look forward to being thrown in with a bunch of bigger girls in P.E."

"Yeah, they're bigger all right." She made an hourglass shape in the air.

I looked down at my own stick figure and grimaced. "That has occurred to me."

"Hey, what time is it?" she asked.

I checked. "Almost four, why?"

"I don't want to miss my favorite talk show. It's at four, so I'm outta here." She got on her bike and started to peddle away. "Just remember," she called over her shoulder. "I vote *no*!"

I picked up the box of vocab words and took out the brouhaha card. Let's see, I thought, what sentence can I make out of this? I know: *The decision to skip the last year of junior high was causing quite a brouhaha in the life of Mary Louise Monroe.* I chuckled.

"Somesing funny?"

My stepdad, Willem, came out onto the porch. He moved to America from Holland three years ago to teach at the university, and he still can't say his *th*'s very well. It bothers him, but Mom and I think it's pretty cute.

"Nothing really funny," I answered. "I was just thinking about things."

"Sinking about what sings?"

I smiled.

4

"It's my *th*'s, isn't it? Dose th's are driving me crazy!" he said. He stuck his tongue out and said slowly, "Thh ... ink ... ing ... about what thh ... ings?"

"Very good," I said. "I was thinking about school and about skipping a grade."

"Yes, that is your big decision this summer, isn't it?"

"Well, I do have to take that test and pass it first," I hedged.

"Ah, I think you'll pass. And I think you know it, too."

"Yeah, I guess if I decide to take it, I can probably pass it. But the test isn't for another week, and then if I do okay, I still have till August to decide for sure."

"Well, it's up to you, but I know I wouldn't give up a chance like that!" He took his car keys out of his pocket. "I have to go over to my office at the university for a bit. When your mom gets here, tell her I'm home soon, okay?"

"Okay, Willem. Tot ziens!"

He smiled. "Very good try at the Dutch, Louise. But remember I told you, *tot ziens* is good-bye for a long time. You should say *tot straks* when someone is coming back. It's like 'see you later.' "

"Oh, yeah. Okay. Tot straks, Willem!"

"Tot straks, Louise!"

I must've fallen asleep, because suddenly Mom was shaking me. "Louise, Louise, wake up."

I opened my eyes and blinked. She looked pale. Like something from the wax museum; like one of the exhibits! I blinked again, but she didn't get any better.

"What's wrong, Mom?"

I sat up and she lowered herself onto the swing next to me. "I just had a call from my mother in Florida."

I tried to picture her mother, but I couldn't. I had only met my grandmother once or twice, when I was real small. Mom didn't want me to spend much time around her because, as the grown-ups said in lowered voices, "Mary Lou has a drinking problem." It had always bugged me a little that I was named after her. I used to worry that I'd turn into an alcoholic, too.

"What does she want?" I asked.

Mom put her hand up to her mouth and pressed her fingers against her lips to keep them from quivering. "She has lung cancer. A large inoperable tumor in her lung that they believe may already have spread to other parts of her body. They don't think she has long to live."

It was like hearing that a stranger was dying. I cared, but not enough to cry. "Oh." I tried to think of something else to say, but suddenly, saying nothing seemed the best thing.

"Where is Willem?" she asked.

Good, here was something I could help with. "Don't worry, Mom. He'll be back soon. He just went over to his office."

"Okay. Well," she seemed flustered. "I have to pack

6

some things and fly down to Florida tomorrow morning. I'd better make some arrangements.'' She stood up and stared at some blue jays fighting at the feeder. ''How do you arrange for someone to die?''

I knew I didn't need to answer, because I knew she wasn't asking me.

Mom went in the house, and I sat on the porch watching the birds. I was still there when Willem got back. I told him what was going on.

''Poor Meg,'' he said. ''It's hard to lose a parent, but even harder when things are not okay between you.''

''Do you know much about all of that, Willem? All I know is that my grandmother is an alcoholic, and that Mom won't let me be around her.''

He shook his head. ''Meg usually loves to talk, but this is one thing she doesn't say much about. I know she had an unhappy childhood, and she doesn't like to discuss it.'' He patted me on the arm. ''Well, I must go see what help I can be.''

The door slammed behind him and the birds at the feeder flapped frantically away.

I went inside. Mom and Willem were having coffee and talking in the kitchen. I poured some iced tea and sat down.

''Well,'' Mom said. ''We can turn my office into a room for her. It's on the ground floor, so it'll be easier for her to get around. While she can.''

''You can share my office, if you like,'' said Willem.

''That will be great honey; *if* I have time to work.

7

I'm not sure how much care Mother will need. I might have to take a leave of absence from the paper.''

Wait a minute! "She's moving in here?" I set my glass down too hard and tea sloshed all over the table.

Mom and Willem looked at me.

"You can't just move her in here. It'll be awful! We were supposed to go to New York City this summer, remember? You guys promised me for my fourteenth birthday. I've been planning for it all year. We have tickets to Broadway shows and everything! Can't we just get a nurse for her or something?"

Mom shook her head. "Oh, Louise."

I sat there awash in sloshed tea and tears. I knew she was disappointed in me, but I didn't care. Parental disappointment is not always a deterrent.

"What do you expect me to say, Mom? Here's this old lady I don't even know and you don't even like, and I'm supposed to be happy that she's coming to live here while she dies? It's creepy."

"Louise, I don't need this right now," said Mom.

"Well, neither do I!" I ran up to my room and slammed the door.

What a brouhaha.

8

CHAPTER
2

"Mom?"

No response.

The "I'm sorry" I had carefully carried with me into her bedroom was stuck in my throat and refused to come out. I think "sorry" is the stickiest word in the English language. "Mom, are you okay?"

She flinched, as if the words hurt. "What? Oh, yes, I'm fine. I just can't decide what to pack, because I'm not sure how long I'll have to stay. It will probably take a week or two to put everything in order and tie up all the loose strings."

I imagined my grandmother hobbling along, the loose strings of her life trailing after her. And Mom scurrying behind trying frantically to tie them into neat little bows.

"Did you get a flight to Florida?"

"Yes, I leave tomorrow morning."

"I hope everything goes okay there," I said. It sounded as lame as I felt.

"Thanks. Me, too."

I went over to her dresser and picked up a wedding photo of Mom and Willem. There they were, grinning like crazy, surrounded by me and all their friends. "How come you didn't invite your mom to your wedding?" I asked.

"I did."

"Didn't she want to come?"

"She couldn't come."

"She couldn't be bothered to come to her only daughter's wedding?"

"It's more complicated than that, Louise. Most things are."

"I know that, Mom. I'm not a baby. I understand more than you give me credit for."

She paused in her packing and looked at me. "Maybe you do." She stared off into space and then said, "She got drunk and missed her flight."

"Oh. I guess that's too bad."

"Yes. It has always been too bad."

"I guess she missed other stuff when you were growing up, huh?"

Mom folded her pajamas and nodded. "Plays, performances, graduations. You name it, she missed it. Except the year she made it to Open House."

"Well, that's one thing, at least."

"Yes, she showed up drunk, threw up on my desk,

and then passed out on the floor of our classroom. The principal drove us home.''

I gasped as I imagined what that must have been like.

''You can see why it's not my favorite subject,'' she said quietly.

''I always wondered why you wouldn't talk about when you were a little kid.''

''Because I see no reason to dwell on it. As I've told you, my father died in an accident when I was a baby, and my mother was an alcoholic. It was very difficult, but it's over now. What's done is done. I can't stand people who sit around and whine about their awful childhoods.''

So, I was right. I always thought Mom must have had a bad childhood. And now she'd admitted it. Not just bad, either, but awful! I was getting angrier and angrier at my grandmother. I have a good imagination and I could picture my mom back then: a small, scared bird of a girl.

''Why don't you just stick your mom in a nursing home, or something?'' I asked.

''Because I wouldn't want to spend my last months in a nursing home, so I can't do it to her. No matter what's happened between us, she is my mother. I guess it never meant much to her, but it means something to me.'' Mom closed her suitcase, then sat down and closed her eyes. ''By the way,'' she said. ''I feel bad about your birthday. I know you were looking forward to your first trip to New York.''

11

"It's not your fault, Mom," I said. I knew whose fault it was; so I asked, "Why did you name me after her? I mean, isn't that supposed to be an honor or something?"

She opened her wet eyes and looked at me. "I hoped if I honored her, she would behave honorably."

The next morning Willem took Mom to the airport. I waved to them from the porch.

"Tot straks!" called Willem.

"Good luck on your test!" called Mom, as they pulled out of our driveway.

"Thanks! Good luck on . . ." I let the sentence blow away. Good luck on what? Bringing an old, dying, lady here, so we could have a death watch? Good luck had nothing to do with this mess.

I went into the house and picked up my vocabulary words. Let's see, the word for today was "insouciance: a carefree lack of concern." I tapped the card and nodded. Yes! Exactly! That's how I would act toward my grandmother: with a carefree lack of concern. I would pay her back for ignoring Mom, by ignoring her.

Then a little voice spoke to me. It's the same voice that reminds me to put money in the Salvation Army pot at Christmas and to volunteer at Special Olympics. The voice asked, *How can you be mean to an old, dying lady?*

I ignored the voice and turned on the TV.

I ate a bowl of cereal and watched Saturday morning

12

cartoons for a while. I don't like the newer cartoons; I always watch Bugs Bunny. I like his insouciance.

The phone rang. It was Anne. "I hope I'm not ringing up too early," she said.

"No, I was just watching cartoons."

"Oh, shall I call back when you've finished, then?"

"No. I've seen these a zillion times. Let's call Becky and go to the pool. I need to get out and do something."

"Right. I'll just fetch my things, and pop over in a quick minute."

"Okay. I'll call Becky and tell her to meet us at my house. See you later."

"Ta-ta!"

We pulled our bikes into the pool at noon, just as it opened.

"Oh lovely! We're the first ones here, so we don't have to queue up," said Anne.

The scent of chlorine mixed with suntan lotion hit my nose. I sniffed. "Mmmmm. The smells of summer."

Becky inhaled. "Yeah, seasons do have their own smells. Like, fall is chimney smoke and leaves."

"And spring is freshly mown lawns," said Anne.

"What about winter?" I asked.

"The damp wool of my muffler," said Becky.

"Stale indoor heat," said Anne.

At the entrance I handed the guy my dollar. "Well, I think winter smells cold and dead. Because that's when everything is—cold and dead and lifeless."

"Oh, well, that's a cheery thought now, isn't it?" said Anne.

Becky shuddered. "Yeah, that gives me the creeps. Let's stop with this death stuff and get outside so we can scam on all the cute boys as they arrive." She threw her stuff into a locker, removed the key and made a beeline for the pool. Anne buzzed after her.

I decided I would have to tell them about my grandmother so they wouldn't think I was some kind of a ghoul. But not now. The old woman might wreck my summer, but it didn't have to start today.

"Wait up, you guys!" I called as I ran to catch them.

I didn't even see Blaise Paradise until I rounded the girls' locker room and smacked right into his chest! A big lifeguard whistle bonked me in the nose.

He grabbed my spindly arms and steadied me. Well, he steadied my body, but not my heart, which was beating like a hummingbird's wings inside my heaving skinny chest.

"Watch out! Remember, no running."

He smiled and let go of my arms. I looked up into his blue, blue eyes and opened my mouth to say something clever and cool.

"Ah, ah, ah, chooooo!"

I sneezed all over Blaise Paradise.

The smile slid off his face. He backed away and headed for the office. Probably to get some disinfectant, I thought.

"Hey, I'm really sorry!" I called, as I watched his quickly retreating, muscular back.

Then Debby Stafford oozed up to him, her bikini straps straining to do their job. After he said something to her, she looked my way, giggled, and handed him her towel.

I tried to act insouciant, which is tough when you're mortified, and made my way over to Anne and Becky. I told them what happened.

After they stopped laughing, Anne said, "Don't get all in a lather. He doesn't even know who you are!"

"He might!" I cringed and added, "I see him sometimes at university faculty family gatherings. His dad works in the same department as my stepdad."

"Did he ever talk to you?" Becky asked, wide-eyed.

"He tried. A little. But I'm always too tongue-tied to respond."

"Oh well," said Becky. "If you *do* go to the high school in the fall, maybe you'll be lucky and Blaise won't remember that you're the tongue-tied girl who spit all over him."

"I didn't spit, I sneezed!"

"Well, I think there's not much difference between the two when you're on the receiving end," said Anne.

Becky squeezed the bottle of suntan lotion and it splurted an extra huge blob onto her leg. She passed some of it around to us.

"Is that really his name, Blaise Paradise?" asked Anne as she rubbed in the lotion.

15

I nodded. "Yes. He even brought his birth certificate to school once to prove it."

"Did you see it?" asked Anne.

"No," said Becky. "He's two years ahead of us. They wouldn't let the seventh-graders look, but everybody else in the junior high school was talking about it."

"Isn't it rather peculiar how people look like their names? He looks like a Blaise Paradise," observed Anne.

Becky pointed her smeared-white finger across the pool at Debby. "And she looks like a Debra Stafford."

"We look like our names, too," I said. "Just ordinary girls."

"Hey, speak for yourself! I'm *extra*-ordinary—in a Becky sort of way." She giggled. "Here comes Evan Simon. He sure looks like his name!"

Evan stopped at our towels. "Hey, ladies! Fending off those harmful UVs, I see." He was wearing an Albert Einstein T-shirt and those geeky sandals that look like they're made out of strips of old tires.

We nodded.

He turned to me and flipped his clip-on sunglasses up. "Hey, Louise, I hear you might be skipping ninth, and heading over to the high school?"

"Yeah, how'd you know that?"

"Because I'm taking the test, too, and I saw your name on the list."

"Oh."

16

He tugged on his bathing suit and Anne started to giggle. He didn't seem to connect his action with her reaction. He just looked confused. "Well, anyway, I'll see you next week. Maybe we can compare notes after the test."

I sat like the sphinx until he disappeared.

"I can't believe that guy. He has always been so weird!" said Becky. "He'll probably want to ride the high school bus with you, Louise!"

"Yes," said Anne. "Perhaps Blaise and Debby will want to join in the fun!"

"Okay, you two twits," I said. "If you've finished, I just have one question. How come guys like Evan walk right up and talk to us, but guys like Blaise Paradise act like we're invisible?"

Becky pulled her hair up into a ponytail. "Because to guys like Blaise, we are invisible."

Her words hit me right in the forehead and I flipped over onto my stomach.

It seems like some people are drawn with a pen: dark, and bold, and hard to miss.

And some of us are sketched in pencil: barely noticeable, and easy to erase. So much for insouciance.

C H A P T E R
3

I saw Evan Simon heading down the hall toward me, so I ducked into the girls' bathroom.

"Oh, nuts! Oh, never mind. It's just some kid." Debby Stafford flicked an ash into the sink and went back to her conversation. "So, I told Blaise that we *have* to go to the big Fourth of July dance at Mountain Lake. I don't give a flying fig if the tickets are fifty bucks. He can cough it up out of his lifeguard salary."

Her friend nodded. Then they both realized I was still standing there.

"What are you looking at? Never seen somebody smoke before?" asked Debby.

I coughed. "No. I mean, yes. I'm just waiting for somebody to go by. Then I'm going to take a test."

"Who asked?" said Debby's friend.

"Who cares?" said Debby.

They cackled and spewed smoke. I decided to ignore

their boorish behavior. I knew it was boorish because that was my word for the day. I peeked out the door. Evan was still lurking.

Debby flushed her cigarette down the toilet and tugged her size M T-shirt over her size L chest. "C'mon, Jen, time to get our butts out there for the tryouts for next year's cheerleaders. I get to show those little rug rats how to do a decent cheer."

Jen looked at me and sneered. "Taking a stupid test on a Saturday in summer? What a geek."

They passed, leaving a wake of perfume, stale smoke, and breath mints. Disgusting.

I slid into a seat in the back of the testing room. Evan turned around and waved. I pretended not to see him. I didn't want him to get the idea that we were going to go to the high school together and be pals, or something. We'd be like a little nerd knot.

I finished a few minutes early, turned in my test, and dashed home. The test was easy. Maybe Mom was right. She'd been ready for me to skip a grade for years; maybe now I was ready.

"Hey, Willem, what are you doing?" I said as I tripped over him on my way inside.

"Fixing a ramp in case your grandmother has trouble with steps, or in case she needs a wheelchair."

I grimaced. That's all I need; death on wheels. "When you talked to Mom, did she say they were bringing a wheelchair?"

"No. But it could soon be that way. It's best to be ready."

"Yeah. I guess so." I sat on the porch swing and watched him.

"So, how was the test? A piece of pie?"

I laughed. "No, it's piece of cake, and yes, it was."

"So, now what will you do?"

"Think about it."

"Sometimes that's the hardest part," he said.

I nodded my agreement and watched him measure wood for the ramp. "It's really nice of you to do all this work for . . . her. Didn't I hear you moving furniture last night, too?"

"Yes. I'm trying to make your mother's office into a bedroom. After all, it's only a few days more until they come home."

"Don't remind me."

He put down his tape measure and looked at me. "I do not understand your anger, Louise. How do you not like someone you don't know?"

"It's easy. People do it all the time," I said.

"Why do *you* do it?"

Suddenly I wished he'd leave me alone. I felt inspected like a butterfly pinned to a specimen board. "I just do, that's all. I don't think my grandmother, if you can call her that, deserves anything from us."

He shook his head and went back to his measuring. "Everybody deserves a good-bye, Louise. It remembers me of my mudder. She died when I was away at university. I wish I could have said tot ziens to her."

"Yeah, well, I bet your mother wasn't an old drunk that ignored you, either." My voice was quavering. "I hate that she's coming here, and I hate that I'm supposed to act all sad and sorry for her, when I'm not!"

I went inside and let the door slam behind me; it punctuated the air with an angry bang.

I flopped on the couch and kicked the coffee table. I saw the family album on the shelf under the table and picked it up. I flipped it open to the beginning. There was just one picture of my mom as a baby, and then the next one skipped her childhood and only showed a photo of her graduation from college. Pathetic. I leaned down to scrutinize the baby photograph.

There was a tall, thin lady standing on a porch. Her dress was all wrinkled. She had a drink in one hand and a baby in the other. The baby was my mom, who looked scared. She was clinging to the tall lady, like she was afraid she'd fall—or be dropped. This was the one and only picture of my mother and my grandmother.

That picture told me all I needed to know.

The phone rang and I picked it up. "Hello?"

"So, how'd the test go? Are you gonna desert me next year?"

"It went fine, Beck. And I haven't decided if I'm gonna skip up, or not. Someone will call in a few days to tell me if I passed for sure."

"But you already know you did, don't you?"

"Yeah. Pretty much."

"Well, congratulations, I guess."

I laughed. "Well, thanks, I guess."

"Was the Simonizer there?"

"Yes, and he was stalking me, so I hid out in the bathroom, and I almost got attacked by Debby Stafford and her fat friend."

"Oh no. That was probably Jennifer Adams. She is so mean. She stole my sister's lunch money for a whole year one time."

"That's awful."

"Yeah, just be warned. Life in high school can be rough, especially without your best friend to stand by your side!"

"Okay, Becky. I get the hint. It's just one more thing for me to worry about this summer."

"One more thing? I thought it was the only thing. Maybe it's that, and wondering whether you'll get asked to the Mountain Lake Fourth of July dance?"

"Hah! I can't think of a single guy who even might ask me."

"I can."

"Who?"

"Evan Simon!"

"Oh, puh-leeez! I'd rather not go."

"My sister says I should just ask some boy myself and offer to pay half. She says if you wait for boys to

22

ask, it takes until the eleventh grade. That's when they can drive.''

''How would you get there?''

''My parents' chariot. But my sister could drive us, so we wouldn't have to be grilled by my dad.''

''Who are you thinking of asking?'' I couldn't believe Becky would be so brave.

''I'm thinking of Blaise Paradise, but I'm always thinking of him.''

''Yeah, you've got lots of company there.''

''I'll probably ask Bryan Binyon. If I ask anybody.''

''Oh. Yeah. He's a nice guy.''

''You're really thinking 'nice nerd,' but what the heck. Birds of a feather, and all that.''

''You're right.'' Pencil-sketched people have to stick together, I thought.

Becky yawned. ''Well, I'm just thinking about it. You know, you should ask someone, and we can get Anne to do it too. After all, it's her last summer here. It would be neat if we all went to the Mountain Lake dance together, wouldn't it?''

''Yeah. It would be pretty cool.'' I paused. ''It would take my mind off the fact that I'm not going to New York this summer.''

''Oh no! How come?''

''Because my mom's mom has inoperable cancer and she's coming to stay with us until it's over.''

''Oh. That's awful. I'd hate it if my Nana was dying.''

"Yeah, that's because you know your Nana. See, you even have a special name for her. I don't even know my grandmother. I don't even like calling her that: grandmother."

"Maybe you could get to know her."

"No. It's too late for that now. Besides, she and my mom aren't even close."

"Oh."

"Anyway, I'm pretty freaked about it, and going to the Mountain Lake dance would be a great way to take my mind off of it. It would probably be the one good thing to come out of this summer of death."

"Don't say that, Louise. It's creepy."

"That's right. It is very creepy."

She sighed. "Well, I'm sorry about your grandma, anyway. If you need to get away or anything, you know you can always come and hang out here."

"Yeah, thanks. I probably will. Listen, maybe we should have a sleep-over with Anne and try to plan some strategy for this Mountain Lake idea. There must be three decent boys in this town willing to go out with us."

"Yeah. At least once, anyway!"

The three of us met at the pool the next day to discuss our plans.

"I think we should each pick a boy and then ring him up during our sleep-over," suggested Anne. She giggled. "My mum would go barmy if she knew I wanted to ask a boy to a dance. She is convinced I'm gadding about and turning into a rotten American teenager. This should push her right over the edge."

"I'd like to push my mom over the edge sometimes," said Becky. "Actually, I guess I have it pretty easy. She's already been through it all with my sister. She just doesn't want me to get drunk or pregnant."

I laughed. "We're worried about even getting one lousy date, and our parents are worried we'll get pregnant."

"I haven't even been kissed!" said Anne.

"Neither have I," I said.

"We have so much in common!" said Becky.

"I would love to relieve my ennui by having at least one date this summer," I said. "And maybe one kiss."

Anne opened a bag of potato chips and passed them around. "Crisps, anybody? And what is ennui?"

I took a chip and smiled. "It's one of my vocab words. It means bored spitless."

"Is that the Webster's definition, or the Book of Louise definition?" asked Anne.

"That's straight from the Book of Louise," I said.

"I'd like to read that book," said a deep voice. We turned to see whose shadow and voice had fallen over us.

I looked up, straight into the eyes of Paradise.

CHAPTER
4

"I still cannot believe that he walked right up and talked to you!" said Becky as she selected a garish red from Anne's colorful collection of nail polish, and then plopped down on the bed to work on her toes.

"I still can't believe he remembered me from those faculty parties!" I said. "I hope he didn't realize I'm the one who sneezed on him." My face flushed at the memory.

"I, for one, shall never forget the look on your face when he asked you to go to the dance," said Anne.

"I, for two, won't either!" said Becky.

I stared up at Anne's ceiling. A British rock star stared back at me. He wasn't nearly as handsome as Blaise. "Just tell me I said 'yes,' you guys, because I can barely remember a single thing."

Becky laughed. "You said something that sounded like 'Glug, maphurg, blitok, oh yes, Blaise, yes!' "

26

"He even knew you were going to be skipping a grade. How did he know that?" asked Anne.

Becky blew on her toenails. "Maybe Evan Simon told him you both passed that test. He's been going around announcing it to anyone who will listen—or anyone who doesn't walk away when he talks to them."

I closed my eyes and pictured the scene at the pool. I remembered Blaise said something about how he hoped I remembered him—as if *he* was forgettable! Then he said he heard I was really smart, and he asked if my name was Laura. I think I told him it was Louise. I hope I did. He said some other stuff, and then he asked me to go to the Fourth of July dance at Mountain Lake.

"Hey, you guys, I did give him my phone number, didn't I?"

Anne nodded and plugged in her electric shaver. "Oh, indeed, you did. Three times."

I buried my head under a pillow. "Oh no. Did I sound desperate?"

"Not really. Just amazed," said Anne over the drone of the shaver.

"What I want to know," said Becky, "is how in the heck you got asked to the ball instead of Princess Stafford. I thought Prince Paradise would go with her."

I came out from under my soft rock. "So did I. So did she! Maybe he got sick of her. I've always thought he was too nice for her, anyway. She's the kind of girl who is mean as a snake when boys aren't around, and then sweet and sticky as cotton candy when they are."

27

"Perhaps he was blinded by her breasts," said Anne matter-of-factly.

Becky and I laughed.

"Actually," I said, "I heard her say she was going to demand that he take her to the dance, no matter what it cost. Maybe he's just tired of her being such a spoiled brat."

"Yeah," said Becky. "A beautiful, bosomy, blond, brat."

"Well, who cares why he asked you? Whatever the reason, Louise, you will reap the benefits!" said Anne.

"I'm so amazed that I'm going with him, I'll be happy to reap just one good-night kiss."

Becky reached for the phone. "Well, I'm going to be happy if I can even go to this stupid dance. Be quiet while I call Bryan Binyon. Absolutely no giggling!" she commanded.

Anne and I held our breaths until she hung up. We let it out in a rush.

"What did he say?" we asked in unison.

Becky started to laugh. "He said he'll ask his mom when she gets home and call me back!"

"Well, take heart, at least he didn't flat out say no!" said Anne between bubbling giggles.

Becky moaned. "I just hope he doesn't want to bring his mother along!"

I woke up the morning of July third and smiled. I had a lot to smile about. I looked at my word for the

28

day, which I taped to my mirror the night before: *Kismet*. So true, so true. It must have been my fate to sneeze on Blaise. Maybe we'd even get married someday.

Blaise was the kind of guy I'd dreamed of marrying ever since I was little. When Becky and I were kids, we played Barbie and staged elaborate weddings. And Blaise was the groom of my fantasies (after college, of course).

Mom sounded tired but happy for me when I told her my good news last night on the phone. "I guess now you won't feel so funny about getting to the high school a little early, will you?" she asked.

"Nooo. Not anymore," I said.

I went to my desk and made a list of things to do:

1. *Clean room.*
2. *Meet B. and A. at mall—get our new dresses for dance!*
3. *Get hair cut.*
4. *Go to airport to pick up Mom and her mom.*
5. *Practice insouciance.*
6. *Hide in room until time for dance.*

I straightened up my room and headed down the stairs to grab some breakfast before malling. I ran into Willem and some wood.

"What's up now, building a new wing onto the house?" I asked.

He smiled. "No. Just some shelves near your grandmother's bed." He rested the wood against the wall. "I'm really looking forward to having Meg back. I missed her."

"Me, too," I said. "What time does their flight get in?"

"About seven. We'll leave around six. Dat okay?"

"Dat's okay," I said.

He smiled. "Thhat's good! Have fun getting ready for the dance. Do you need any money for the party dress you will wear?"

I blinked back unexpected tears. It was such a fatherly thing to ask me. At least I thought so, since I've never had a dad around, and I wasn't sure.

"I saved up some baby-sitting money. I was gonna use that," I said. I learned to be frugal during the lean years with Mom.

He reached out and tentatively patted my hand. "Well, maybe you'll let me help some. I would like to do this for you. Remember, you're the daughter I never had."

He wiped his hands on his work pants, pulled out his wallet and handed me some money.

"Thanks," I said quietly.

He nodded, picked up the wood and walked away from the hug that neither one of us knew how to give.

"Ah, Willem?"

He stopped and turned.

"How do you say 'I love you' in Dutch?"

He put down the wood and walked back to me. "Like dis." And he gave me my first, genuine, father's hug. It was nice. Safe and warm, and smelling of sawdust and sweat.

Anne and Becky piled our packages on a chair while I went to get three Diet Cokes. The mall was jammed. It used to be packed only in December; now it goes on all year. Mom says it's because people are too lazy to think of anything else to do.

"I am dead angry with my mum," Anne said as I handed her the drink. She sucked on her straw and continued. "First, she refused to allow me to tarnish the family name by asking a boy out, then she told me she had got me a date for the dance with a smashing fellow who goes to military school. Well, I met him last night." She sucked again.

"And?" said Becky.

"And, he's an oaf with a crew cut."

"Oh, maybe he'll be nice," I said. "Those boys from the military schools usually know how to dance really well."

"I don't care if he has two left feet! I wanted him to be drop-dead gorgeous! Besides, you wouldn't understand, you're all set with your little trip to Paradise."

I smiled contentedly.

Becky counted her money. "Anybody want a burger or fries, or something? I'm gonna get something to nosh on."

31

"Okay, I'll queue up with you, if you go to the loo with me," said Anne.

"Okay. Louise, watch our junk and don't dream of Paradise too much!"

"Har, har, you two crack me up. Go on, I'll guard the stuff. Bring me back a yogurt, will you?" I handed her a dollar.

Opening the bag, I peeked at my dress. It was so pretty: pale pink with tiny flowers and a high bodice. It was a little old-fashioned, but then, so was I.

I imagined dancing with Blaise and walking in the moonlight near the lake and having fun with Anne and Becky and their dates. And I imagined my favorite part: a wonderful, warm, good-night kiss from Blaise. I felt my face flush and my toes tingle. Mmmmm, Paradise.

I blinked back to reality because someone said my name. "What?"

Debby Stafford and Jennifer Adams sat down across from me.

"I hear you're going to the dance with my boyfriend." Debby picked up my Coke and took a swig. "You don't mind sharing, I'm sure," she said.

I swallowed the lump in my throat.

"You know," Debby continued, "for somebody so smart, you're pretty stupid."

"I am not stupid," I said with certainty.

"Oh, yeah? Then ask yourself why a popular hunk like Blaise would ask a flat-chested, fourteen-year-old freak to a dance when he could go with me, or any other girl he wanted. Any single girl in the whole town. Why you?''

I shrugged. "He just likes me. Maybe because I'm not like you.''

Jennifer snorted. "That's for sure.''

Debby reached over and pulled my dress out of the bag. "Oooooo. Isn't this pretty? So pink, and prim, and proper.''

I grabbed for the dress and she held it just out of reach. "I won't hurt your geeky little party dress, Cinderella. I just wanted to see if I was right.''

"You were right,'' said Jennifer.

"What? Does she train you to parrot things like that, or do you just speak in echoes?'' Anne glared at Jennifer and Becky grabbed my dress from Debby.

"You little British witch!'' said Jennifer.

"Jennifer, I'm going to tell your mother,'' said Becky. "I'm sure she'd be ashamed of you.''

"I'm sure she already is,'' I said.

Debby laughed and stood up. "Oooo. What a comeback! C'mon, Jen, don't waste your breath.'' She turned to me with narrowed eyes. "Just ask yourself, Cinderella, Why me? Why would he ask you to this dance? There must be some reason. See if you can figure it out. I'm going to the dance too, so I'll be watching.''

She waltzed off and Jennifer trotted after her. I could almost hear her whinny.

"Whew!'' said Becky. "I thought they were going to beat the snot out of us.'' She handed me my dress.

33

Anne laughed. "I'm suddenly glad I have a military escort to this dance tomorrow!"

I carefully folded the dress and put it back into the bag. "Thanks, you guys. I should have said something to her, but I was so shocked . . ."

"Don't worry about it," said Anne. "Bullies are scary whether they're boys or girls."

That night, driving to the airport, I was pretty quiet.

Why *did* Blaise ask me to the dance? Was Debby right? Was there some hidden reason? I hoped it was because he wanted to date a nice person, for a change. Maybe he finally saw the quiet beauty of a person sketched in pencil.

"Are you thinking about your dance or worrying about your grandmother coming?" said Willem as he pulled the car into a parking space and turned off the engine.

"Both," I answered.

Mom and her mom were the last people off the plane. I stood aside and waited for Willem to finish hugging Mom. I snuck a peek at my grandmother.

She was not as tall as I thought, and she was very thin. She eyed me, eyeing her.

"Got a cigarette?" she asked.

CHAPTER
5

"Oh, Mother, please!" Mom looked over Willem's shoulder and shook her head.

"Margaret, you have always been such a stick in the proverbial mud. I was just kidding." My grandmother winked at me.

I didn't feel we were on winking terms yet, so I spoke to my mom. "How was your trip? Everything go okay?"

"Yes, it went fine, considering. We got most of mother's things squared away."

"Sold away, you mean." The old lady turned her attention to Willem. "Would you believe she sold my 1968 Cadillac? We could easily have driven it up here, and then I would still have some semblance of independence." She stuck out her hand. "You must be Willem. I'm Mary Lou, your mother-in-law. At least, what's left of me is."

Willem grinned and gently shook her hand. "I'm very happy to meet you. Can I be of some help to you? Shall I tell the skycap to order for you a wheelchair?"

"Heck, no! Let me walk while I still can! But I'll tell you one thing, Dutch, you are okay in my book. I can already tell you're a big improvement over that moron Margaret took up with the first time around!"

Mom shushed her and nodded toward me.

I was all ears. My real dad was another subject my mom was completely clammed-up about. Not that it mattered all that much. Once, in grade school, the counselor tried to counsel me about not having a dad. I told her that all the kids I know had dads and color TVs. I didn't have either one. It might be nice to have them, but if you don't, you adjust. She let me go back to class.

"Oh, for God's sake, you mean to tell me you haven't told the kid anything about her own father?" The old woman shook her head and started to cough. "Excuse me. My lungs are exacting revenge for forty years of smoking," she said when she had recovered. "Anyway, Margaret, this just takes the cake. You have got to be the most secretive person I have ever met!"

Red seeped into Mom's face. "Well, perhaps I had very good reason for that!" She shifted her carry-on luggage to her other shoulder and redirected the conversation to safer ground. "Let's head for the baggage area. We've got plenty."

Willem stuck out his arm for Mary Lou to lean on

and she smiled. "Dutch, you and I are going to get along like two peas in a pod!"

Two out of four isn't bad, I thought. I'm still on Mom's side.

We loaded the stuff into the car and headed home. Mary Lou sat up front with Willem. Whew.

"We had a heckuva few weeks, didn't we, Meg?" She didn't seem to need an answer—and Mom didn't seem to have one—so she continued. "After I got over the initial shock of the diagnosis, I just wanted to clear things up and get out of hot, sticky Florida. That's God's waiting room down there, you know. A big herd of senior citizens just waiting for the grim reaper to call their number. Hah! But not for old M. L. I'm in ol' Virginny. And you know what? I intend to live long enough to see the leaves change! That will be something."

Willem looked at Mom in the rearview mirror. She shook her head no.

"When do the leaves change, anyway? When I was a girl in Pennsylvania it was around September, I think."

"Well, Mother, in Virginia it's usually in October." My mom cleared her throat. "That's a good three and a half months away."

"I can count, Meg. I'm dying, not dead. And I intend to see the leaves change. I think dying wishes are usually granted. Even the dying wishes of old drunks."

Silence settled over the car. Willem lifted it. "In the

Netherlands the leaves don't change. They just get brown. It's nothing people would get in their cars and go driving around to look at, like they do here.''

"Speaking of cars . . .''

"Let's not,'' said Mom.

"Lets,'' said Mary Lou. "I still don't see why we couldn't get my Caddy up here. It would come in handy. This way, if I want to get out I'll have to bother you or Dutch.'' She turned and looked at me. "I guess you're too young to drive?''

I nodded.

"Are you too young to talk too?''

This boorish old lady was starting to shake my insouciance.

She turned back to the front. "Probably just like your mother. I can't even believe she and I are related sometimes.''

"Neither can I,'' I mumbled.

"You mumble just like her, too,'' she said. "Margaret and I are like night and day, aren't we, Meg?''

Mom closed her eyes and leaned her head back. "Yes, Mother.''

I patted Mom's hand on the seat between us. She opened her eyes and smiled small. She leaned over and whispered, "She's the one dying, and I'm exhausted.''

I nodded. It looked like I was going to have to be more involved than I thought. It was pretty clear that Mom couldn't handle old Mary Lou all alone.

I dropped my attention back into the front seat. *She* was talking about the stupid leaves again.

"I've heard that the leaves will be just brilliant this year; something about a cold snap early in the year that makes the leaves brighter in the fall. Is that right, Dutch?"

"I'm not sure, Mary Lou. Maybe Louise knows something about it."

"What about it, namesake? You learn anything about the leaves in your science class?"

Namesake. That was getting harder and harder to swallow. I sat forward. "Not that I recall." Actually, I recalled plenty, but I wasn't about to tell her.

"Too bad. Maybe I'll just have to make a trip to the library and check it out myself."

"You do that," I said.

"I've always loved the library. I've always been a voracious reader. You know what 'voracious' is, namesake?"

I sat up straight. "Of course I do. It means you like it so much, you consume great amounts."

"Aha—a fellow reader. I thought so. Well, like it or not, namesake, we seem to have something in common."

"That's just great." I felt like a well-read fly caught in a web of words.

We pulled into the driveway and Willem helped Mary Lou up to the porch swing. We unloaded the luggage.

39

"Is this all?" he asked.

"No, Dutch," she called from the porch. "Meg left some of my things in storage in Florida."

Tattletale, I thought.

Willem looked at Mom. She leaned against the car.

"Well, she had some stuff in storage for years. I forgot about it until the last minute, so I called the place and the guy said he would send the stuff UPS. He said it was just a few old boxes. I hardly think it's important. She said she didn't want to leave without it, but she can't even remember what it is."

"Well, then, let's just get her inside and settled into her new place. The boxes will come when dey come." He gestured to me to open the door.

Willem led Mary Lou down the hall into her room. It looked good. He had arranged everything carefully so it would be comfortable.

She sighed, sat down on the bed and swallowed some pills. Willem explained the television remote and the VCR. He showed her how to raise and lower the blinds and how to work the radio. "I want most of all for you to have comfort here."

She smiled at him and removed the card from the tulips he had ordered. "Welcome home," she read aloud.

He beamed.

"Well, Dutch, you're not the first man to make me cry, but you are the first man who ever gave me flowers." She smelled the tulips and pulled a tissue from

40

the box by her bed. "Better late than never, right?" She forced a laugh. "So. Enough of this maudlin nonsense. Just point me to the bathroom and let me use it while I still can." She wobbled a little and grabbed the doorjamb. Willem sprang to steady her.

"Hmmm. I hope this doesn't keep up. I'm determined to avoid the indignity of the bedpan!"

"You're just tired, Mother." Mom helped her across the hall. "Don't worry about bedpans."

She closed the door. "Easy for you to say. All you'll have to do is empty it."

That didn't sound easy to me.

Mom rolled her eyes. "I just can't win with her. No matter what."

"You go to bed. I'll see to it she gets settled." Willem hugged Mom and patted her behind. "Go on! Let the Zs catch you."

Mom giggled. "You are my sweet Dutch treat."

"I know. Tot straks." He winked.

Mom giggled again.

"You two are bonkers!" I said.

Mom smiled and kissed me on the cheek. " 'Night, Louise. Thanks for coming along."

"Can I come with you while you take off your makeup? I want to tell you about Blaise and the dance and everything."

"Can it wait till the morning, sweetie? I'm dead on my feet."

The bathroom door opened. "No you're not. I am.

41

Almost.'' Mary Lou chuckled and headed back to her room.

I kissed Mom and followed Willem into the death room.

He put away her things and adjusted the thermostat. ''Well, if you don't need anything else, I'll be seeing you tomorrow. Good night and tot straks!''

''Tot who?''

''Tot straks is Dutch for 'see you later.' ''

''Well, I sure hope so!''

I started to follow Willem out.

''Hold on, namesake. Let me have a word with you.''

Willem nudged me back into the room and closed the door.

''What?'' I stood stiffly near the escape hatch.

''I know you don't want me here.''

''I don't care where you are.''

She folded her arms. ''Have a seat. I'd offer you a drink, but I gave it up.''

I stood my ground. ''It's about time.''

She picked up a pencil and held it like a cigarette. She looked at her hand. ''Old habits die hard.''

''Lots of things die hard,'' I said.

''Score one for you.'' She leaned back and smiled. ''Well, you might not want to hear this, but I've changed my mind. You're not like your mother. I think you're more like me.''

My silence sat like a rock in the middle of the room.

42

She ignored it and continued. "Looking at you is like looking at myself in 1941. You sound like me too."

I put my hand on the doorknob. "I am nothing like you."

"You are like me. And a little like your dad, I think. Around the eyes."

"No. These are my eyes. And I know what I see."

"Believe me, namesake. You can look right straight at something and not see what it really is. Appearances are deceiving."

"Yeah, tell me about it. Kind of the way you raised my mom, huh?" I opened the door, closed it, and went to bed.

CHAPTER
6

I sat on the couch and bounced my knee. I checked my purse and straightened my hair. I felt like an already leashed dog, waiting to be walked. If I had a tail, I'd be wagging it. "Was that a car in our driveway?" I catapulted from the couch and knocked some books off the table.

Willem looked over his newspaper. "*Potverdikkie!* Sit down, Louise! You'll know when he is here. He will ring the bell."

I smiled. "Are you swearing at me, Pop?"

He grinned over the paper. "Did I receive a promotion to 'Pop'?"

I nodded.

"Well, I wouldn't swear at my daughter. Even in de Dutch. It just means, ahh . . . let me think of the Engels. . . . I guess it means, 'oh shoot'!"

Mom came in with the camera. "What's going on in here?" She picked up the books.

44

"Louise is bonkers, I think," said Willem.

I nodded.

"Well, try to relax. I know you're excited, but try to calm down. You'd think you had a date with the king of England."

"Might as well be a king, as far as I'm concerned." I adjusted my bodice and wished I was zaftig; which was, so far, my absolute favorite vocab word. Who would ever guess it meant full-bosomed?

"That's my point, dear," Mom continued. "He's only human. Just like you."

"I'm not so sure about that. Wait till you see him."

She rolled her eyes and fiddled with the camera. I heard crunching gravel and flew to the door.

"Louise!" Willem shook his head. "Bad form for you to open the door. Let your mother get it."

"Okay, Pop." I slunk to the couch and tried to breathe calmly. The bell rang. Mom opened the door. She brought Blaise in and introduced him to Willem.

Blaise seemed to take up the whole room. He was tan skin, blond hair, and white teeth—all wrapped up in a blue sport coat and khakis.

Willem shook his hand. "Well, Blaise. I'd like you to look after my girl. After all, this is her first date . . ."

Oh No! Don't tell him that! I tried to scream with my eyes, but Willem went on fathering.

"I expect her to be treated well and to be returned home at a reasonable hour."

No! I want to come home at an unreasonable hour!
said my eyes.

Blaise smiled and the room lit up. "Yes, sir. Of course. I'll take excellent care of her. My older brother will be driving us tonight, and we'll be home after the fireworks, before midnight, if that's okay?"

Willem nodded, flushed with his newfound father power.

"That'll be great, Blaise," said Mom. "How about a quick photo of you two, ah, over by the fireplace?"

Blaise smiled and I glowered. Then I felt his arm go around my waist. My skin prickled up and the hair on the back of my neck joined in.

"Okay, smile!" chirped Mom.

We were just about out the door when it happened.

"Hey, namesake, don't I get to meet the hunka, hunka burnin' love?"

I nearly fainted.

"Oh, now, Mother," said Mom in a rush. "The kids were just leaving."

"I can see that. I'm not blind. I just wanted to see young love in bloom." She smiled and readjusted her T-shirt. It had flamingoes dancing all over the front of it. I wanted to break their skinny flamingo legs.

Blaise put out his hand. "Pleased to meet you, ma'am. I didn't realize Laura had such a fun family."

Her eyes narrowed. "I've been around the block a few times, young man. And I can see you are as smooth as silk. My granddaughter's name is Louise. And where is her corsage?''

"Oh, so what?" I bleated nervously. The last thing I was worried about was a stupid flower and my name! "Let's go, Blaise!" I pulled him toward the door.

"Well, it was nice meeting all of you. I'll have Louise home nice and early."

Not if I can help it, I thought.

"Listen," I said as we walked to the car. "I'm sorry about all of that, I . . ."

He took my hand. "No sweat. I thought your family was cool. Your grandmother is a real laugh, and it's nice how your dad checks up on things. It's kind of old-fashioned."

I looked up gratefully into his handsome face and melted into the backseat.

"This big goon is my brother, Morgan." Blaise jerked his thumb toward the front seat.

I smiled. "Hi, Morgan. Thanks for driving us."

"Hey, no sweat. I'm going stag tonight, so it's no prob." He started the car and backed slowly out of the driveway, under the fatherly eye of Willem, who had come out onto the porch.

Mountain Lake is reached by a long and winding road. As we approached the top, it was like entering Oz. The old stone hotel, draped in light and color, was reflected in the lake. I *ooh*ed and *ahh*ed, in spite of my efforts to be insouciant.

Morgan laughed. "It's awesome, isn't it?"

"It looks like the Emerald City in the Wizard of Oz," I said.

"Wait till the fireworks, then it's really something!" He turned off the ignition and turned to me. "Did you know they filmed a movie up here last summer?"

I nodded.

"Blaisey boy and I actually got to be extras in that. Did he tell you?"

"Wow! Really? No, I didn't know." I looked at Blaise and sighed. Movie star, sort of.

Blaise opened my door and helped me out. "It was no biggie. You can't even see us. We didn't have any lines, or anything."

I smoothed my dress and took his offered arm. "But still, that is such a cool experience. I read that they were casting for extras, but I was taking an honor's summer school course, so I couldn't try out."

"Yeah, well, not me! I get enough school during the year." He grabbed my hand. "Let's head for Oz and party!" He pulled me toward the light, the noise, and the night. I followed willingly.

I've walked into rooms full of people before, but heads never turned the way they did tonight. It was all because of Blaise. He's one of those people drawn in pen—with such a flair and a flourish. I was just happy to be a sketch by his side.

We checked my wrap and headed for the ballroom. "You dance pretty good," he said later.

I blushed. I knew he was being polite. I was just sort

of moving carefully to the music. "I guess it's all those years of practicing in the living room."

We danced three dances, and I was getting thirsty. "Do you think we could get a drink?" I yelled over the next song.

He nodded and grabbed my hand. I could feel his confidence shoot up my arm. "I'll take you outside to the pier. They have tables set up out there, and a gazebo for dancing. It's much cooler." He found us a table and asked what I wanted.

"A Coke would be fine. I'm going to run to the ladies' room, then I'll come back here, okay?"

"Okay. Hurry back, and don't you dare leave this spot," he ordered. "I want to be able to find you." He grinned and touched me under the chin.

"I want to be found."

He nodded and left me.

I spotted Becky and Anne and their dates and waved them over.

They arrived in a wave of laughter and perfume.

"Hey, where's Paradise?" asked Becky.

"And where's your corsage?" asked Anne.

"Oh, I didn't want one," I lied. "Doesn't this place look wonderful?"

"It's grand!" said Anne. "By the way, Louise, this is Jonathan Warren, my escort."

"Good evening," said Jon, in his best military manner.

I smiled and nodded. "Why don't y'all sit down?

Blaise will be right back. He went to get drinks. And I was just going to the ladies' room.''

Anne looked at Jon. ''I'm parched, actually. Would you fetch me a drink, while we go to the loo?''

''Oh, of course. Hey, Bryan, let's go round up some drinks for the ladies.'' Jon gazed down at Bryan, who was gazing at Becky.

''Bryan! Listen up!''

''Huh? Oh yeah, drinks, okay, I'm coming.''

They marched off, Bryan bringing up the rear.

Becky laughed. ''Well, that's a relief. If he doesn't stop staring at me, I'm going to scream! I feel like he's memorizing every freckle on my face!''

We went inside and found the restroom.

''God save the queen! This place looks like Buckingham Palace! And it's just a loo!'' Anne giggled and sat down on the chaise lounge.

Becky ran her fingers over the wallpaper. ''This stuff feels like velvet. It's fancier than my dress!''

We ogled the decor and headed for the stalls.

''So, how's it going?'' I asked.

''Smashing, thanks! I'm having a lovely pee!'' Anne said through the wall.

''Har, har. You know what I mean. The dance!''

''Well, it's lovely here, but I'm beginning to wish Jonathan would push off. He keeps driveling on about his military academy and what a fine institution it is. It's bloody annoying.'' She flushed just as I did, and then we washed our hands. Anne took off her shoes

50

and rubbed her feet. "I thought you said those military blokes were marvy dancers. If he treads on my toes one more time, I'll swat him a good one!"

I laughed. "Well, I heard they were very polite and good dancers. Anyway, I'm having a great time. Blaise is, is, just so . . ."

Becky called from inside a stall, "I can't believe it! Miss Vocabulary is at a loss for words!"

"It's a bloomin' miracle," said Anne.

"He's so masculine," I said. "It's as simple as that."

Becky came out and smiled as she washed up. "Nothing is that simple."

I leaned over the sink and reapplied my pale pink lipstick. "I just hope he kisses this lipstick right off my face!"

Someone inside another stall laughed. We exchanged embarrassed looks. The door of the stall opened. Debby Stafford emerged.

"Well, well, well. Kiss the lipstick right off your face, huh? That's real cute." She sashayed over to the mirror and ran her tongue over her lips. "I never wear lipstick. Blaise hates it."

I swallowed and wished I could think of something clever. Debby seemed to drive my cleverness to the attic of my brain.

Anne jumped in. "Bugger off, you cow."

Debby reached into her purse and pulled out a pack of cigarettes.

51

Becky pointed at a sign. "You probably can't read. That says, NO SMOKING."

Debby lit up. "I don't follow the same rules you little trolls follow."

I started to cough. "Let's just go, you guys. I can't stand being poisoned."

Debby swung on me and grabbed the front of my dress. She shoved me into the paper towel holder. "Listen, creep. You might have him tonight. But it won't last, believe me. He'll get what he wants and then he'll drop you. You don't know him like I do. You've got something he wants. He's just trying to figure out how to get it."

Becky grabbed Debby's arm. "Let her go."

Debby let go. "Sure." She smiled. "No harm done." She looked at me. "Good thing you didn't get a corsage, I might have smashed it. Funny, you're the only one here whose date didn't bother to buy her a corsage. Wonder why?" She dragged on the cigarette and put it out in the sink.

"I didn't want one," I said. My voice shook when I said it.

She looked at herself in the mirror and ran her fingers through her hair. "Yes, you do. This is your first big date, and you wanted a corsage like everyone else. You wanted to press it in some stupid book, and take it out and blubber over it for years to come." She gestured at my friends. "You might fool them, but you don't fool me. You think because I don't get good grades, I'm stupid." She readjusted her corsage. "There's lots of ways to be stupid."

"Yes, and you're so cunning, you've managed to collect all of them." Anne grabbed our arms and propelled us out the door.

We got back to the table and the guys were there. All except Blaise.

As we approached, Jon jumped up and pulled out a chair for Anne.

"Please do sit down. I'm not Princess Diana," she said.

"Just being polite," he said politely. "By the way, Miss Monroe, your date asked me to tell you he'll be back momentarily. He had to talk to some guys on the varsity football team."

Bryan sucked loud at the bottom of his glass. "Yeah, he said they had some tips for him about how to get onto the team for sure. He'll probably make it. Guys like him always do."

Becky smiled. "Sure they do, Bryan, but so what? You're on the debate team."

He smiled. "Yeah, we knock brains instead of bodies."

Jon suddenly popped up again.

Debby smiled. "My, what a gentlejerk—I mean, gentleman."

"Sit down, Jonathan," said Anne. "That's not a lady."

Debby laughed and sat down. "That's right, I'm not.

What could be more boring?'' She pointed at me. ''Besides maybe being you.''

''What is it, now?'' I asked warily. My head was still smarting from the whack in the bathroom.

''I forgot to tell you one important thing. I know you think Blaise just used me for my body, but he's just using you for . . .''

''Get out of here, Deb.'' Blaise walked up and pulled her chair out. ''You're bothering my date. Go find your own date, I'm sure he's sniffing around for you.''

She stood up and smiled at him. ''Don't worry. I didn't tell.''

''How could you?'' he asked. ''There's nothing to tell.''

She shrugged and readjusted her straps.

The lights lowered and the band started a slow dance. ''Come on, Louise,'' said Blaise. ''Let's dance.'' He grabbed my hand and led me out to the gazebo. ''She didn't bother you, did she? She's kind of jealous—because we used to go out and stuff.''

''I know,'' I said. I snuggled down into his arms and swayed to the music.

''What did she say to you?'' he asked quietly into my hair.

''Nothing important. She said you took me out because you want something from me.''

He moved us expertly through the crowd of dancers. ''Well, she's right.''

I jerked my head up.

"Can you blame me? I have had my eye on you for months. I want to go out with a cute, smart girl for a change. That's something." He smiled down at me and brushed his cheek over my forehead. "My dad says he heard that you're so smart, they're gonna let you skip a grade. I bet you don't even get nervous before exams and stuff."

I nodded into his jacket. "Yeah, school has always been easy for me."

"That's what I thought. I've always wanted to date a smart girl," he murmured.

I sighed. Who cares about mistaken names and missing corsages? I leaned in closer and fell in deeper.

C H A P T E R

7

Morgan maneuvered the car carefully down the hill. "So, did you guys have a good time?" He didn't wait for an answer. "We'll have you home by eleven-thirty, Louise. Blaisey boy said your dad wanted you home early."

"Not *that* early," I protested. "I mean, I hope you guys aren't having your evening ruined, or anything, because of me."

Blaise yawned. "Nah. I've got football tryouts tomorrow. I should hit the sack."

Blaise and Morgan talked about how fireworks work the rest of the way home. I probably could have explained it to them, since I had some going off right inside of me.

"Oh, would you turn up this song?" I asked.

"Sure thing." Morgan reached over and twirled the radio knob.

It was "Oldies but Goodies Night." I sat back and closed my eyes. They were playing a love song.

I thought the lyrics spoke right to Blaise and me. It was all about how these two very different people get together, and everyone says it will never work. I looked over at Blaise. He didn't seem to be hearing it the way I was. He and his brother were discussing sparklers.

The closer we got to town, the sweatier my palms got. I wondered if Blaise would kiss me at the door. Probably not. After all, it was a first date. As the car took the curves and their voices rose and fell, I was aware of every square inch of him on the seat next to me. Sometimes the car would swerve sharply, and his thigh would press against mine. Little shock waves shot through my body and set off new fireworks. What I really wanted to do was lean my head against his shoulder and have him hold me and kiss me, just like in the song on the radio.

"Back, safe and sound!" said Morgan, as he pulled into our driveway. He grinned over the front seat. "Go on, little bro, walk her to the door." He chuckled. "I'll even close my eyes."

Blaise slugged him on the shoulder. "Ignore my big brother, the big jerk." He got out and opened my door.

I thanked Morgan and walked slowly toward the house. The porch light—which had been a dim bulb when I left—was now illuminating with about a million watts. Willem's handiwork, no doubt.

I put my hand on the screen door, but didn't open it. "I had a great time, Blaise," I said.

"Me, too." He grinned down at me and brushed the hair off his forehead. "That's quite a spotlight you've got there." He nodded toward the blazing bulb.

"I think my stepdad just installed that tonight," I said apologetically.

He smiled and shook his head. "Yeah, big, bad boyfriend detector."

"Maybe it's just to protect the daughter from the dark," I suggested.

He chucked me under the chin and turned to go. "Maybe. But I like to kiss in the dark."

I was about to offer to claw the light out of the ceiling when he said, "Well, see ya around, Louise."

"When?" I asked anxiously. I bit my tongue. It sounded kind of desperate.

He stopped halfway down the path. "Don't worry, I'll let ya know." He smiled. "I know where to find you. I'll just follow the sound of the sneezing."

I came to a quick, full boil of embarrassment. "Oh no. I hoped you didn't realize that was me."

He laughed. "Of course I knew. We've already shared a sneeze. We're practically engaged." He shoved his hands into his pockets, sauntered to the car, slid in, and rolled away.

"Mom!" I yelled as soon as I got inside the door. There was no answer, so I charged into the dark kitchen, bashed into the table leg and yelled, "Potverdikkie!"

The light switched on over my head.

"Well, young lady," said my grandmother, "I'm glad it's just you returning from your date with Blast. You just about jarred my peaches! Nearly scared me to death—which wouldn't be hard since I'm hanging around at its doorstep!" She sat down and laughed at her morbid joke. "That was pretty good, don't you think?"

I rubbed my shin and went to the fridge. "No, I don't think. I don't see how you can make jokes about death all the time. I think that makes it harder for everybody. And his name is Blaise, not Blast." I got out the iced tea and poured a big glass. I raised the pitcher and my eyebrows at Mary Lou. She nodded, and I gave her a glass.

We sat in uncomfortable silence for a few minutes. The refrigerator hummed and the ice maker churned out baby cubes.

"So, where's Mom and Willem?" I asked.

"At the fireworks display. They weren't going to go and see the stupid things just because I'm moored here. I told them to get out of the house while they still can. No need to sit around and watch me like an hourglass that's been upended." She sipped her tea and coughed. She kept coughing.

"You okay?" I asked.

"Oh, yes. I'm bright-eyed and bushy-tailed. It's my lungs that need to be dry-cleaned." She coughed again.

"Did they go to the community fireworks at the park?" I asked after she recovered.

"I have no idea. It took me an hour to convince them that I didn't want to go with them. After that, I was just glad they were gone."

"Why didn't you go?"

She smiled and adjusted her flamingo T-shirt. "Well, I just didn't have a thing to wear, my dear."

"No, really. After all, it might be your last . . ."

"My last chance to see fireworks?"

I nodded and felt bad.

"I've been on the planet for nearly sixty-five years. I haven't seen fireworks up close yet. I don't think I need to start any new traditions now. I just want to see the leaves change this fall. Once more, for the road."

I took off my shoes and put my feet up on the chair across from me. "How could you not ever have seen fireworks?"

"Well, it wasn't hard. When I was a little girl, they didn't do fireworks displays, except in the big cities. And later, in the orphanage, they only let us watch from behind the wall. And we couldn't really see."

I stopped rubbing my feet and looked up. "Orphanage?"

"Yes, the orphanage where I lived from the time I was eleven until I was old enough to support myself— around sixteen, or so. I lived there during most of World War Two."

"You lived in an orphanage?" I still couldn't believe my ears. "Like in *Oliver Twist*?"

She laughed. "Well, not quite that bad. Things had improved since Dickens's time. Besides, I believe old Oliver did time in a workhouse."

"Oh. I had visions of you asking for more gruel."

"No, they didn't starve us. We got lumpy Cream of Wheat."

"How come nobody ever told me about any of this orphanage stuff?" I asked. "Does my mom know about it?"

She nodded. "She knows some."

"But not much, I bet."

"That's right. I see no reason to moan and groan about my life in the orphanage. What's done—"

I interrupted her. "Is done, right?"

She nodded.

"You sound *just* like my mom," I said. "You two do have something in common: you clam up about your past." I sipped my iced tea and held the cool glass to my forehead. "I think it would be better to talk about this stuff."

"Just remember, namesake, clams are hard-shelled and closed tight for a reason." She stood up and looked around for her glasses. "Where are my eyes?"

"They're hanging on that chain around your neck," I offered.

She smiled. "Well, you know what they say: the eyes are the first things to go!"

I pulled my feet off the chair and stood up. "Especially in this family!" I rinsed our glasses and shoved them into the dishwasher.

"Hah!" she said on her way out. "We've got our eyes wide open. We just happen to be standing in the dark."

I switched off the light and followed her. I figured I should at least make sure she made it back to her room.

I watched her struggle with the caps on her pill bottles. Obviously, my plan for insouciance was going to have to be revamped. I opened the pill bottles and helped her get ready for bed. When she was all settled, I brought her some water so she could take the little army of pills.

"I thank you kindly, Louise," she said. "I can surely use this sleeping pill."

I nodded and leaned against the wall. "You know, I just can't understand this orphanage stuff. How did you end up there?"

She clicked the light off near her bed. I now leaned in the dark.

"I don't like to discuss it," she said. "It was a long time ago. A lifetime ago."

"Okay, fine. If there's one thing I'm used to, it's people not talking about their past. Keep your story to yourself." I started to close the door behind me. Her voice came thinly through the darkness.

"My mother died when I was ten. I was the oldest of the five kids. My father tried for a while, but he decided he couldn't handle us, so the next year he put us all in an orphanage. My sister Cecelia and I were separated from our brothers. The end.''

"I'm sorry," I said.

"Don't be. It wasn't your fault."

"I know that. But I'm still sorry it happened to you."

"Well, I don't want pity. I have found that people who need pity are usually pitiful."

"It's not pity, it's . . . ah . . ." I scanned my brain for a vocab word. "It's empathy, and that's a whole different thing."

She laughed and yawned. "You remind me of Sister Catherine, a nun at the orphanage. She always used to say, 'Remember, Mary Louise, you have a choice in life. You can be a stone or a cork.' Then she'd drop a stone and a cork into a glass of water."

I smiled in the dark. "So, you decided to be a cork, huh?"

"No, my dear, it's quite obvious. I wanted to float, but I couldn't, try though I might. I sank slowly and settled sadly at the bottom of a bottle of booze."

I stood quietly for a little while and blinked back tears of empathy. "Good night," I paused, then added, "Grandmother."

But she was already asleep. It was just as well.

I waited for Mom and Willem in the kitchen. When they came in, I pounced on them and told them all about the dance, minus the Debby stuff.

63

Mom yawned. "That's wonderful, sweetie. I'm glad your first date went so well, even though Blaise forgot the corsage. Did Mother get off to bed with no trouble?"

I yawned. "Yes. It was fine. I helped her get ready for bed. We even had a little chat."

Willem yawned. "Good thing for you, Louise. I told your mother we could count on you."

I smiled. "Yeah, and I can count on you, Pop, to keep that porch light shining bright."

He grinned. "I have to be more careful for you, now that I'm Pop."

My Mom got up and kissed me good night. I grabbed her hand. "Did your mom ever tell you much about the orphanage?" I asked.

Mom stepped back. "She told you about that?"

I nodded.

"I'm amazed." She sat back down. "Actually, I don't know much . . ."

"That's no surprise," I interjected.

She frowned at me and continued. "Just that her mother died and her dad couldn't cope. All five kids were put into an orphanage. Her father tried to contact her later, but she wouldn't speak to him. She never spoke to him again."

"How'd her mom die?"

"Some type of cancer. Her mom was a nurse, did you know that?"

I rolled my eyes. "Well, how could I? Nobody tells anything around here."

Mom looked at Willem. "I'm off to bed. You coming?"

He nodded. "I'll be there directly."

She kissed both of us and left.

Willem sat down next to me. "I'm proud of you for helping with your oma."

"That's grandma, right?"

"Oh, yes, I mean grandma. It's good to talk to people before they are gone."

"Like your Mom?"

He nodded. "Like dat."

"I guess I don't mind talking to her, but she doesn't seem to want to talk very much."

He stood up and patted my shoulder. "Maybe it is sometimes that people don't talk much because they are not asked much."

I shrugged. "I don't know. In this family, it's a tradition not to talk. I don't know if asking will help."

"Yes, you do know. You are a smart daughter."

I buried my head and my smile in my arms. "Okay, okay, Pop. You win. I'll ask more."

He smiled from the doorway. "Louise?"

I looked up.

"Ik houd van jou."

I looked and looked at him. I lit up. "Oh! I love you, too, Pop."

Some things don't need to be translated.

CHAPTER

8

"Louise, you must come over to my place, straight away!"

I shifted the phone. "Well, Anne, I can't for a little while. My mom has been hounding me to make a decision about skipping up. Ever since they called and said I passed, she has been on full nag. So, I'm sitting here, making a list of the pros and cons . . ."

Anne cracked her gum in my ear. "Well, mop up all of that and get over here!"

"Why so vehement?" I was pleased to get to use my vocab word so early in the day.

"Oh, will you let up on those daft words of yours? This is dead serious."

I closed my notebook. "Okay, okay. Is Becky coming too?"

"Natch. Get a move on. And straight away!"

I stared at the phone as I hung up. What could possibly be going on to ruffle Anne's English feathers?

I jumped at the sudden jangle of another call. I held my breath; maybe it was Blaise. It had been three days since the dance. . . .

"Hello? Louise speaking." I tried to sound sophisticated.

"Hello. This is Nurse Simon from the local hospice. I'm trying to reach Mrs. Meg VanderVeen."

"Just a moment, please. I'll get her."

I found Mom in her mom's room. They were arguing—again.

Mom was standing in the middle of the room holding a plate of vegetables and steamed fish. "Now, Mother, Doctor Tyler told me you have to eat things that are fresh and healthy. You need to keep up your strength."

"I don't *have* to do anything but die and pay taxes. Why should I keep up my strength? I have no plans other than to see the leaves change this fall. And you can drive me around for that. Just give me a minute steak and some instant potatoes. I'm in no position to wait for elaborate menus."

I chuckled. I couldn't help it. The old lady kind of grew on me. It was like when I first met Willem and he wanted me to try this Dutch soup called Erwtensoep. It's really thick, really putrid-colored pea soup, with floating lumps. It looked to me like something somebody threw up. It smelled yukky too. I knew I'd hate it. But when I finally tried it, it wasn't too bad; not what I was used to, but not bad. Now I eat it all winter long.

"Hah! See, namesake gets my jokes better than you

67

do." She jabbed the air with her pencil and picked up her crossword puzzle book.

Mom shook her head. "Fine. You are so obstinate! I'll fix you some instant oatmeal and some minute rice."

I saw her mom smile.

"Mom, there's a nurse from the hospice on the phone. She wants to talk to you," I said.

"Good. What a relief. The cavalry is coming." She looked at the fish, tsked at her mother, and went to answer the phone.

"Did you know she called the hospice?" I asked as I straightened her pillows.

Mary Lou put down her puzzle book. "I'm the one that made her call. I saw how well it worked in Florida; I worked at one for a while as a secretary. I figured your mom could use a break. Hospice nurses step in when things get really bad. And I'm not likely to get any better."

"Hospice is the nurses that only take care of dying people, right?"

"Yes. I think I qualify, don't you?"

"I don't know. Except for the coughing, you seem pretty lively to me. Maybe you're not as sick as they thought?" My hopeful words settled over us like a down comforter.

She smiled. "Don't you go counting on miracles. I don't qualify for those."

I looked at her thin, nervous hands. "I don't know, maybe you do."

A wave of compassion washed over me. I felt a strong undertow pulling me toward my grandmother.

She looked out the window and waved me away. "What are you doing hanging around in here on such a beautiful day, anyway? Don't you have some gallivanting around to do?"

I remembered Anne's call. "Yes, actually, I do. I'll see you later, okay?"

"You'll see me. And if you don't see me, you'll hear me. I do not intend to 'go gentle into that good night.' "

I smiled and quoted the end of the poem. " 'Rage, rage against the dying of the light.' "

She nodded and gazed out the window. "The light can't die until I've seen the leaves change."

"You will," I said with certainty. *"Tot straks!"*

I ran upstairs, put my bathing suit on under my clothes, grabbed my backpack and headed for Anne's house. I intended to go to the pool afterward and see what Blaise was up to (and who he was up to it with).

Anne opened her door and yanked me inside before I even had the chance to knock. "What took you so bloody long?"

Anne's mother popped into the room. "Anne Elizabeth, would you please mind your language? I'm not raising a guttersnipe." She nodded at me. "Good afternoon, Louise. Lovely to see you again, dear."

"Hi, Mrs. Clarke. Thank you for having me over."

She wiped her hands on a towel. "Oh, it's always a

pleasure. I'm just about to open a tin of tuna. Will you stay for a bite of lunch?''

I looked at Anne.

She grabbed my arm and pulled. "No thanks, Mum. We've got gobs of things to do. Becky will be here soon; have her pop up, will you?''

I laughed and followed her upstairs to her room. We walked down a hallway covered with pictures of Anne as a baby. "I love these pictures," I said. "Ladies and gentlemen, to your left and right we have, Anne: the drooling years."

"Stop blithering, Louise. Get in here and sit down."

"Geez, Anne! Why are you having such a cow?"

"I wish I were having a cow, as you so quaintly put it. It would be preferable to what I actually had."

I sat on her bed. "I'm in a quandary. What's up?"

There was a kick on the door and Becky came breathlessly into the room, carrying a tray of drinks. "Your mom sent these up. Did I miss anything? Did you tell her yet?''

Anne shook her head solemnly and gestured toward the bed. Becky passed out the Cokes and plopped down.

I shook my head and looked at them. "Will you two puhleeze tell me what in the heck is going on? You are acting like junior high school spies!"

Anne jiggled the ice in her glass. "Has Blaise called you since the dance?''

"No."

"I thought not."

"Why?" My mouth went dry and my heart skipped a beat. I took a swig of Coke.

Anne threw a pillow down on the floor and sat cross-legged at my feet. "Well, yesterday my family took an excursion to the park. I was mad with boredom, as usual, so I trotted off to feed the ducks. Suddenly, I heard a great deal of merriment issuing forth from a park bench, just beyond some shrubs." She paused to drink some Coke.

I swallowed and waited for her to continue.

"I decided to investigate. So I poked about, parted the leaves and came upon Blaise Paradise and Debra Stafford."

Becky patted my hand. "Anne says they were in a bit of a clinch."

"Are you sure, Anne? Are you sure it was him?" I could feel my heart sink like the *Titanic*.

Anne nodded. "Not a shred of doubt, I'm sorry to say. It was the golden couple."

Becky put her arm around me. "You know, Louise, guys like that are pretty slick. My sister says Morgan Paradise is the same way. She says he has a dating rap sheet about a mile long; a lot of the really popular guys do."

I leaned my head on Becky. "I just can't believe it. He was so sweet to me. I thought I knew what he was like."

"Well, I would like to have booted his bottom directly into that murky duck pond, that's all I can say,'' said Anne.

Becky patted my hair. ''I think you were out of your league, Louise. They play hardball when it comes to boyfriends and stuff.''

I sat up, pulled my towel out of my backpack, and wiped the tears away. ''Look, we don't know for sure. It's easy to misjudge people. Maybe there's some explanation. You know how Debby is. Maybe she lured him there with some lie . . .''

Anne snorted. ''Oh, indeed. And then she forced him to plop down on that bench and entwine himself around her. That's a likely story.''

''Were they kissing?'' I asked quietly.

''No, not while I was observing them.''

''Well, then come on,'' I bleated, hanging on to my shred of hope. ''We really can't be sure. Will you guys come to the pool with me, so I can maybe find out what's going on?''

''Of course,'' said Anne.

''You bet,'' said Becky.

''Okay, then pack up your junk and let's go.'' I wiped my nose and shoved my towel into my backpack.

''Don't forget to pack your nerve,'' said Anne.

We got to the pool in record time and set up our stuff in our spot. It's weird how everybody stakes out their own special spot at the pool, just like they do at school. Ours was in the far corner, where we could observe and comment on all romance, bathing suits, and diving techniques.

I put on my shades so I could search unobserved for Blaise. He wasn't in his lifeguard chair or at the baby pool. "Beck, will you go to the lifeguard station and see if he's on break?" I asked.

"Sure, no prob. Do you want me to tell him you're looking for him?"

I thought. "Well, ah . . ."

Anne shook her head and stuffed her hair under a baseball cap. "I wouldn't advise it, Louise. Just have her check if he's about. Best to act as if you don't care too much."

"That'd be acting all right," I said. I got out my suntan lotion and carefully wrote—squirted—B-l-a-i-s-e on my belly. I rubbed it in and waited.

A shadow fell over us and I looked quickly up. Then quickly down. "Oh. Hi, Evan," I said leadenly.

"Hi, Louise." He dropped his book on my foot and bent down to retrieve it. "Sorry."

I nodded and rubbed my foot. Leave it to Evan to bring a humongous hardback to the pool.

"So, are you going to the high school in September?" he asked. "I am. Definitely. I think it's best to take these classes as soon as possible, and then get going on your college career . . ."

He was as annoying as a gnat. "Listen, Evan. I'm not sure what I'm doing yet, so don't go around telling everybody I've skipped, okay?"

73

"Oh, I haven't. I just told them you passed the test. I thought it was great that we both passed together."

He made it sound like we'd had a baby or something. "Anyway, Evan, I don't mean to be rude to you, but I'm here with my friends, so . . ."

"Oh, yeah, okay." He started to leave, then he turned back. "Ah, Louise, I just wanted to say I'm sorry about your grandmother."

I jerked my head up and pulled off my shades. "How'd you know?"

"Well, my mom's a hospice nurse, and she had her schedule out this morning, and I saw your address. So I asked her, and she said your grandmother is ill."

My attitude softened; my voice lowered. "Yeah, she is. Thanks for asking about her, Evan."

He offered a lopsided smile, gave the Boy Scout salute, then plodded away.

"He's rather nice for a nerd, isn't he?" asked Anne.

I nodded but didn't answer because Becky was jumping towels and dodging kids to get back to us. She ran up, panting.

"Well?" I demanded.

She nodded. "Chill, I'm getting to it. Just let me breathe for two seconds."

"One, two, your time is up. What's going on?" asked Anne.

Becky flung herself onto her towel and breathed. "Okay, he's off today . . ."

"Oh, bloody hell," said Anne.

"But," Becky continued, "one of the other lifeguards knew where Blaise was going tonight."

"Where?" we asked in unison.

Becky smiled. "He's going to The Third Eye around ten o'clock, to hear some band."

Anne whistled. "My mum mentioned that club not long ago. She claimed it was some den of evil—and warned me never to set one delicate English toe across its threshold."

I leaned in and put my arms around their shoulders. "So. Who is interested in a sleep-over at my place, and a little trip downtown, around ten, or so?"

Becky smiled. "I think we're about to get a look in The Third Eye."

"Exactly!" I said vehemently.

C H A P T E R

9

"Which one should I wear?" Becky stood in front of my full-length mirror and dangled two T-shirts for our approval.

"That black one is rather peculiar; I'd wear it," said Anne.

I nodded. "Yeah, I think it's bizarre enough. After all, we don't want to look like three junior high kids."

"In that case, I think we'd best apply a bit of makeup," said Anne as she rummaged through her purse. She produced bottles and tubes of assorted cosmetics. "Come along! Time to disguise our youth. We musn't let our spots shine through. Acne will be a dead giveaway."

I wiggled into my jeans mini and pulled on a T-shirt. "Listen, you guys, I told my parents we're taking the bus downtown to a late movie at that student-run place that shows old classics. They'll pick us up outside the theater around midnight."

"What's playing?" asked Becky as she put blue gunk on her eyelids.

"*Casablanca.* Have either of you guys seen it?"

Anne nodded and nearly poked her eye out with the mascara wand. "I've seen it on the telly. It was lovely."

"I've seen it too, so if they grill us, we're safe. Anne and I can fill you in on the plot, Beck." I sucked in my cheeks and put blush on what stuck out.

We sat and looked at ourselves in the mirror.

"I look like a clown," said Becky.

"I don't look like a proper English young lady," said Anne. "I look like a tart! What fun!"

"I look like a little girl who got into her mother's makeup," I said.

"Well, then, we're ready to take a peek in The Third Eye, isn't it?" Anne stood up and put the makeup back in her purse.

"Okay, let's sneak out quietly, so my parents don't see how we look. We can wipe this stuff off before we come back home." I got some money out of my baby-sitting pot and stuck it in my purse. "Let's get going before I wimp out."

When we got to the kitchen I stopped to write a note to my mom.

Someone coughed. Becky and Anne jumped.

"Hey, namesake, what are you three up to? No good, I'll bet." My grandmother walked slowly over to the table and carefully lowered herself into a chair. "Hello, ladies. I'm Louise's grandmother, much to her dismay."

Anne laughed. Becky went right over to her and sat down.

"Hi, I'm Becky. I'm Louise's best friend."

They shook hands. "Pleased to meet you. I'm Mary Lou."

Anne joined in. "Hello there, I'm Anne Elizabeth Clarke, visiting from Great Britain."

"Veddy nice to meet you my deah," said my grandmother.

"Listen, we'd love to chat," I said hurriedly. "But, we really have to get going . . ."

Mary Lou put on her glasses and eyed us suspiciously. "Get going to do something that you're not supposed to, and that you're terrified your rule-following mother will find out about?" Mary Lou coughed and took some pills out of her pocket. She asked for iced tea.

I slithered over to the sink, like a lying snake, and got a glass.

I set the tea in front of her. "Are you going to tell on me?"

"On us," corrected Anne.

"No. But I do intend to blackmail you." She coughed and continued. "I want you three to tell me why you are painted up, where you are going, and what you plan to do when you get there. Take your time. Your parents just went out to the store."

We looked at each other.

"We're going to a movie," I stammered. Now my vocab word made sense; lying is not my forte.

"Hah! Never lie to a liar, Louise. You three remind me of myself, Molly, and Inez in 1944. The clothes, the hair, and the war paint are different, but the more things change, the more they stay the same, I always say. We were always up to something."

Becky poured herself some tea. "Like what?"

"I'll bet you were a real corker," said Anne.

I rolled my eyes and gestured at the clock, but Anne and Becky were already being sucked in. I clomped over to the table and sat down.

Mary Lou laughed at some cobwebby old memory and continued. "Well, I could tell you about the time the three of us went to see Frank Sinatra; except we could only afford one ticket!"

"How'd y'all get in?" asked Becky.

"Well, we were in line outside the theater with about a million other girls. They called us bobby-soxers back then."

" 'Cause you wore those short socks, right?" asked Becky.

"No, because they were all named Bobby," I said sarcastically. They ignored me.

"Do go on," said Anne.

"Well, we had only been able to scrape up enough money for one ticket, so we talked the guy at the door into letting us share one seat. We cried and fumed and fussed and held up the line, and finally he said, 'Ah, shuddup, and git inside and gawk at the skinny creep! Just stop holdin' up the line.' " She smiled and shook

79

her head. "If you girls think Elvis was big, or the Beatles, you are sadly mistaken. There was never anyone as big as Old Blue Eyes. He was the first singing idol. We were all crazy for him and we'd swoon and scream, 'Oh Frankie, Frankie, we love you!' " She leaned back and hummed some old tune that was carrying her back in time.

Anne hummed along.

"How do you know this song?" asked Mary Lou.

"My mum volunteers at a club for wrinklies, and she makes me go along. They demand his music."

My grandmother laughed. " 'Wrinklies'?"

Anne blushed. "Oh, well, I didn't mean to offend. That's what the kids call the senior citizens back home."

"I'm too wrinkly to be offended!"

"So what happened back at the concert?" asked Becky impatiently.

I sighed and looked at my watch.

"Well it was the cat's meow, as we used to say. Molly, Inez, and I shared that one seat, taking turns standing on it to see him, and afterward we tried to get backstage to get a glimpse of Frankie."

"And did you succeed?" asked Anne.

"I did."

"Really?" I asked. Now I was caught up in the tale, like a fish in a net.

She nodded. "There was such a crush to get backstage that I got separated from Molly and Inez. I was

80

skinny, so I could squeeze through where bosomy girls couldn't." She grinned at me.

"Did you really meet Frankie?" asked Becky.

"Yes, sort of. He came out of his dressing room, just as I got there. For a second I stood there, scared spitless. Finally I recovered enough to sputter, 'Oh, Mr. Sinatra, you were the end! The real end!' " She laughed. "I couldn't think of anything else to say, and I didn't have a program for him to sign, so I just dangled there."

"What happened!?" we asked.

She smiled at the memory. "He smiled, patted my behind and said, 'Thanks, baby.' Then he walked away between two bodyguards."

"Wow," breathed Becky. "How cool."

"That's not all," she said.

"It isn't?" asked Anne.

"No. I figured I had nothing to lose, so I screamed, 'Frankie, I love you!' "

"What did he do?" I asked, oblivious to the time.

"He stopped and turned around."

"Oh my gosh, what did he say?" asked Becky.

"He said, 'Take a number, baby. Take a number.' Then he blew me a kiss and strolled away." She drank some tea and hummed her old tune.

"That is fabulous!" said Anne.

"I agree," I said, wondering what other stories my grandmother was hiding in her shell. I looked at my watch. "But we absolutely *have* to go."

"Where to, to do what?" asked my Sinatra-loving grandmother.

I sighed. "Okay. I'll tell you. We're all dressed up so we can get into a club downtown called The Third Eye. We want to see what Blaise is doing. We heard he'd be there."

She yawned and rubbed her neck. "He's probably making time with some waitress." She looked at me and shook her head. "I can tell there's no use in talking to you; you're infatuated up to your eyebrows. You three go ahead, but stick together and stay out of trouble. Don't try to order a drink, because they'll I.D. you, and then you'll be up the crik without a paddle."

Mary Lou stood up. "I'll go back to my room now, but I want to hear all about this tomorrow. Assuming you three don't land in jail."

We helped her to her room, and I kissed her goodnight. She was kind of talking to herself when we left. I heard her say, "Good old Molly and Inez. I wonder what ever became of those two? Remember when Frankie sang 'All or Nothing at All?'"

I clicked the door shut.

"She's really something, that old girl. I don't know why you were so worried about her coming here, Louise," whispered Anne.

"That doesn't matter anymore. Now I'm worried about her leaving," I said.

They nodded and we went quietly down the hall. It was time to go.

The Third Eye was located behind a Laundromat, and then down some steep, fungus-covered stairs. I thought I saw mushrooms growing in the cracks. There was a big old, ugly eye painted on a sign. It hung and creaked by one hinge over our heads.

We passed through a beaded doorway, went inside and found a table. Which wasn't easy, because it was dark enough in there to develop film.

"Interesting decor," said Anne when we were seated on some stools that teetered around one of those giant spools that hold telephone wire.

I nodded. "Did you notice the bats? I'm pretty sure I saw a couple hanging in the stairwell."

"I think I see a few hanging around in here," said Becky. "Only they're sitting at the tables."

"I recognize these people," said Anne. "This is the same crowd that emerges for Earth Day once a year, isn't it? They must go back underground the rest of the time."

Becky giggled. "Yeah, that's when they do all that tie-dyeing."

A ponytailed waiter strolled up. He was wearing a tie-dyed T-shirt. Becky laughed.

"What do you guys want?" he asked.

"What do you have?" asked Anne.

He sighed. "Salads, vegetarian sandwiches, lotsa herbal tea, and we got coffee, and we got beer, but you guys can't have beer."

I straightened up. "Why not?"

"Because, you're, like, too young."

"How can you tell?"

He pointed at me: "Training bra." At Anne: "Baby fat." At Becky: "Retainer."

"Oh." I wound myself around my spool. "Okay, we'll have three herbal teas."

"Cool." He meandered off into the darkness.

"*What* fat?" asked Anne as she examined her arms in the dim light.

I patted her hand. "Calm down. You just have sort of chubby cheeks."

Becky popped her retainer out with her tongue. "Well, he got me right."

I sat up straight. "He got it all wrong for me. I am *not* wearing a training bra. I can still get away with an undershirt."

Anne pouted. "Well, he's a cheeky twit, if you ask me. I am certainly not keen on this place."

I made a face. "Oh, don't worry about him. Who pays attention to a guy who wears an earring in his nostril?"

Anne laughed. "So true. How on earth does he blow his nose?"

"Yeah, maybe boogers get stuck in it," said Becky.

"Boogers? What a disgusting term. Can't you think of something more refined?" Anne asked.

"Oh, yeah, like boogers are refined. What would you call them in the UK?"

Anne thought. "Actually, we don't refer to it. If we did, I suppose we'd say nostril debris."

Becky cracked up. "I am really sure, Anne."

"Come on, you guys, enough booger talk. Let's get serious. We've got work to do." I squinted and tried to see in the dark, but my eyes still hadn't adjusted. "Can either of you see anything?"

"No way. You get more light from a firefly than you do from these groddy candles," said Becky.

Pierced nostril returned with our tea.

"Pardon me," said Anne. "But we were informed that there would be a band playing here tonight. Is that correct?"

He gave her a funny look and set down the tea. "Uh, yeah. The Stags are playing, but they don't start for another fifteen minutes. Plus, they play in the back room, where the dance floor is." He gestured off into the back blackness of the cave. "You can go back if you want. A lot of people are hangin' out back there already."

Anne sipped her tea. "Thank you so much. You've been most informative."

He scratched his nose and disappeared.

We sipped the tea and tried to see in the dark.

I looked at my watch. I could almost see it. "Okay, I think it's been about fifteen minutes, let's go check out the back room."

CHAPTER
10

We wended our way between broken tables and sandaled feet.

"What is that weird music?" asked Becky, looking up at some huge speakers.

"That's Indian music," said Anne. "There are lots of people from India back home. I hear that sitar stuff all over the place."

"It's kind of neat, actually," I said as I stepped over a box of crystals.

The guy at the table looked up. He held up a long chain with a twirling crystal. "Hey, you chicks want to buy a crystal? They promote positive energy."

"I already have a necklace," said Becky.

I shook my head and smiled.

"No, thank you very much. My mum thinks they are evil," said Anne. She pulled on us to continue.

He shook his head and went back to his positive energy work.

We giggled and held on to each other until Anne stopped short. We piled into her like an accordion.

"We have arrived," she said. "Louise, would you like to go first? You're probably better at spotting Paradise than we are."

I nodded and led the way. "At least there's a bit more light in here," I said as I searched, like a lighthouse, for Blaise. I was successful. I shone my beam on him.

He was standing down front and over to the side with what looked like the entire football team from the high school. They were laughing and jockeying for position near the stage.

I pointed.

"Aha," said Anne. "They seem to be celebrating. He must have made the team."

"Those guys are such hunks," said Becky. "Mom says they're hormones on feet."

"I'm going over there. You guys wait here." Anne started to protest but I ignored her and pushed through the crowd. I only had a little bit of bravery, and it was sinking fast. I kept my beam on Blaise and steamed ahead.

He didn't see me, but I could see him clearly. He fake-punched one of the guys and laughed. He shook his head and ran his hand through his hair. He was wearing faded jeans, an open-necked plaid shirt, and a cloak of confidence. I walked up and tapped him on the arm. He turned and looked down at me. At first he looked puzzled, then he cracked a sunny-side up grin.

I smiled. "Hi, Blaise. Remember me?"

He grabbed my elbow and steered me away from the crowd. Again I felt his confidence surge up my arm. We stopped in a darkened hallway that led to the kitchen and the bathrooms. A voice from the kitchen called for more tofu.

"Hey, Louise, am I ever glad you're here," he said.

I smiled, happy that he got my name right.

He chucked me under the chin. "Listen, I was going to call you tomorrow to tell you that I made the varsity football team!"

I squealed and jumped up and down. "Oh, Blaise, that is so great, I'm so happy for you!" I threw my arms around his neck and hugged him.

He laughed and patted my back. He stepped back and looked at me. "Thanks a lot, but it's not quite time for us to celebrate." He took out some gum and popped a stick in his mouth. He waved the package at me. I shook my head. "There's one small catch," he said.

"What?"

"Well, they passed a C-minimum grade rule a few months ago." He chewed his gum and looked at me.

"What does that mean?" I asked. I had no idea what he was talking about. I never pay attention to sports.

"It means that I can't play unless I pass two equivalency tests next month. One in English and one in math."

"I don't understand, why—"

He interrupted. "I'm not proud of it, but I barely

passed those classes. I got a D in both of them. I'm not sure what to do. I really have to pass those tests." He shook his head and rubbed the back of his neck. "I shoulda been paying more attention, but things were always going wrong with Debby. She always had some crisis, and it made it hard to concentrate at school."

I furrowed my brow. "Are you still seeing her?"

"Nah. She keeps coming around, but I'm trying to let her down slowly." He smiled at me. "I'm interested in someone else now."

I blanched. He meant me. "Listen, Blaise, I think I could help you get ready for those tests. I already took algebra and geometry in an accelerated math program, and English is a piece of cake for me . . ."

He grabbed me, picked me up, and swung me around. "You are so great! I can't believe you'd give up half your summer just to help me."

I held on tight as I got dizzier and dizzier. But I had no intention of letting go.

Anne pulled her sweater around her shoulders and looked up the street for our van. "Wasn't that band bloody awful?"

"They were the skankiest looking guys I have ever seen," said Becky. "Didn't you think so, Louise?"

"Mmmm hmmm," I said.

"There is no use in speaking to her, she is absolutely blotto about her close encounter with Blaise." Anne waved her hand in front of my face. "See? She is blinded by lust."

Becky laughed. "You better wipe your mouth off, Louise. You missed some of the lipstick."

"Perhaps Blaise smudged it with a good-night kiss," said Anne.

I shook my head and wiped my mouth on my sleeve. "No. No kiss. I think he's waiting for a better time and place."

"Well, he won't have to wait long, by the looks of you," said Anne. "You know, I think you should watch your p's and q's with him, Louise. Are you sure he's not just using you for some free tutoring, with the intention of dropping you as soon as he passes? And it did not look to me at the duck pond as if he was letting Debby down slowly, regardless of what he claims now."

"Look, Anne, you don't really know him. I can tell he's not like that. He's already talking about how we can go out after the football games next fall."

Visions of crisp fall air and me cheering Blaise from the stands danced in my head.

Becky stuck her head in. "Does that mean you're definitely going to skip a grade then, to be with him?"

I smiled. "Yeah, I think it's time."

"Thanks a lot, pal."

"Listen, Beck, it's not just to be with him . . ."

"It's just mostly, that's all," she said.

The van pulled up and we piled in.

"Hey," said Mom. "How was the movie?"

"Great," I lied. "We had scads of fun."

Anne and Becky echoed.

"Good," said Willem. "I'm glad to hear you girls had fun."

I slunk down. Lying made me feel small.

"So," said Mom cheerfully, "the hospice nurse came by this afternoon."

"Oh? How'd it go?" I asked, glad to be able to talk about something else.

"I think it was good for my mother to have someone else to talk to and good for me to have a break."

"I liked your mom, Mrs. VanderVeen. I met her tonight," said Becky.

"I did, as well," said Anne.

Mom turned around. "Thanks, girls. I'm glad you got to meet her. She is certainly unusual. I have to admit, I haven't always gotten along with her. When I was your age she seemed like such an embarrassment."

"I can relate," said Becky. "My mom could give lessons in how to totally embarrass your daughter. You know what she does when she can't find me in a department store? She doesn't go and get me paged, like a normal person. Nooooo. She wanders up and down the aisles hollering, 'Rebeeeeeca, Rebeeeeeca!'"

Mom and Willem laughed.

"My mum and I have terrible rows sometimes," said Anne. "I question my paternity at times."

Willem smiled. "Yes, Anne. Perhaps they found you

floating in the Thames, and you're really a royal princess from the Netherlands."

"I wouldn't doubt that at all," said Anne. "It would certainly explain my younger brother's lack of refinement."

Becky laughed. "You *sound* like royalty."

I closed my eyes and my ears and thought about Blaise until we got home.

Willem locked the door and turned off the porch beam. "Good night, girls. Tot straks!" he called as we climbed the stairs.

We got ready for bed and turned off the lights.

"Becky, you're not mad at me, are you?" I asked.

The moon shone into the room, and I saw her turn toward me in her sleeping bag. "Not really. I guess I just feel like you're picking Blaise over me."

I sat up and rested on one elbow. "Yeah, but if you had the same choice, wouldn't you do the same thing?"

"I guess," she said. "Maybe."

"I know something," said Anne. "You don't choose between them, you choose both of them. Boys don't have to come between you two. I think we need our boyfriends and our girlfriends."

I plopped my head back down. "Anne, I think you're right about all that, but wrong about Blaise. It's easy to mistrust someone for all the wrong reasons."

"Perhaps," she said. "But it's also easy to trust them for the wrong reasons."

We talked for a little while, then I could tell Becky and Anne were asleep.

I went over everything Blaise had said and done. He was so sweet and so sincere. I knew Anne had to be wrong about him. After all, I had been wrong about my grandmother. . . . I heard something and sat up straight in bed. I heard it again. A noise from downstairs; like something breaking. I got up and stepped carefully over my friends. I padded to the door and opened it a crack. I heard someone crying. I slipped out the door and headed for the stairs.

I found my grandmother on her hands and knees, trying to clean up a broken vase.

"Grandmother, it's me, what happened?" I knelt down and touched her arm. She shook her head. Her hand was bleeding.

I helped her up and made her sit on the bed. I ran and got some Band-aids. I came back and bandaged her hand and cleaned up the water, flowers, and broken glass.

I went to sit by her on the bed but she stopped me. "It's wet," she said quietly.

"How did the flower water get . . ." Then I knew. "Oh, it's okay, don't worry about it. I'll clean it up." I started to strip the bed but stopped when I heard her sob.

"Look at the new nightgown Dutch gave me, it's soaked." She clutched at the tulip-covered material and stared at her feet. "I don't want to be a burden," she said in a choked voice.

My eyes puddled up and I patted her back. "It's okay. No one has to know. I'll start the laundry now, and I'll put it in the dryer tomorrow morning. Nobody will ever know." I helped her put on a fresh nightie, and I stripped and remade the bed. She sat in her rocking chair and watched me.

"There," I said. "Good as new."

"Far from it," she said. "This will happen again, you know."

I nodded. "When I was seven, I still wet the bed. Mom used to wake me up in the middle of the night to use the bathroom so I could be dry in the morning. We could try that."

"That will only help for a while," she said. "Besides, I don't relish the idea of disturbing your sleep every night for a lavatory rendezvous."

"But I don't mind," I said.

"But I do." She got back into her bed and sighed. "I've always been very independent. The one thing I've dreaded the most was the bedpan. I just can't handle that. I don't want anyone to have to do that for me."

"But when you first came, you made jokes about it . . ."

"Better to laugh than to cry, I always say."

"Oh."

"I appreciate this, namesake. I owe you one."

"Well, I'm going to come down tomorrow night and wake you up. I don't care what you say."

She laughed. "Yes, that's the ticket. Ignore an old dying lady's wishes."

I smiled. "Well, I want to do it. It might work for quite a while. You never know."

"Nope, you never do," she agreed. "But I think I'll tell your mother. She'll ask about my hand, anyway, and I'm too tired to come up with a clever story." She pulled the covers up close and leaned back. "So, as long as you're here, what happened at the Open Eyeball?"

I laughed. "It was The Third Eye, and it went great. Blaise was not with some waitress, and I'm going to help him study for some exams this summer. And he's going to get me a good seat to watch him play football and we're going to go out afterward, and—"

"Whoa, Nellie! What's this about exams?"

I squirmed. Why did everybody jump on that part? "Well, he needs help to pass some exams this summer, so he can meet the C minimum needed to be on the team."

"And you're the lucky gal that gets to tutor him, huh?"

I nodded.

"Does he at least get your name right now?"

I defended him. "Of course he does. Give the guy a break. That was our first date, he was nervous."

"About as nervous as a snake in a hen house. They know what they want, and they know how to get it. Swift, smooth, and silent."

"You're wrong about him. You'll see," I said.

"So, did he kiss you good night, yet?"

"No. See? Doesn't that prove he's not a creep?"

"It either proves he's not a creep or that he's a very careful creep."

I rolled my eyes.

She laughed. "Boy, that reminds me of a kissing rhyme we used to recite."

"What?"

"Kissing spreads disease it's stated; kiss me, kid, I'm vaccinated!"

I laughed. "Maybe someday I'll get a kiss."

"Well, when you do, I hope it's from someone you can trust."

I decided to change the subject. "Would you like me to read to you, like Willem does?"

She nodded. "Yes, that usually takes my mind off the grim reaper and all his little surprises." She pointed at a big, ancient book of poetry on her nightstand. "We've been reading from this."

I picked it up and I read the next few poems. "These are such good poems. Not like the stuff we read at school. Where'd you get this book, grandmother?"

She opened her eyes. "From my mother. She gave it to me two days before she died. I suppose she knew it was time for final gestures."

"She died of cancer, right?"

"Yes. And, apparently, it has become a family tradition."

I closed the book. "I wish you wouldn't talk like that," I said. "You shouldn't give up."

She was silent.

"So, what happened when your mom died?"

"Well, people didn't go to the hospital much in those days, and she had been sick at home for quite a while. Late one night she asked me to go and fetch the doctor. My father worked the railroad and he was gone all the time; so the oldest had to go. I remember running over the cobblestone streets, and how cold the air was through my nightgown."

"Did you get help?"

"Yes, I brought the doctor back to our house, but he made me wait in the kitchen. He came out and told me she was gone."

"I bet you missed her," I said quietly.

"I still do," she said.

CHAPTER
11

"Are you going over to Blaise's house again?" My mom looked at me over her shoulder.

I waited for her to turn back to the sink. "Uh-huh. It's really no biggie, Mom. We just study together." I halfheartedly shoveled salad into my mouth. That part was certainly true. All we did do was study and talk a little bit. And we'd been doing it for weeks. Sometimes I even met him at the pool and we studied on his breaks.

"Well, I just wanted to be sure you weren't being a nuisance to Mrs. Paradise." She arranged some fruit on a plate and fixed a tray for my grandmother.

I pointed at the tray. "She won't eat that, you know. She wants salty, fattening, fast-food junk."

"I know that. But I have to try to get a few decent meals into her." She picked up the tray and headed for the door.

"Why don't you let her have what she wants, Mom? What difference could it make now?"

She banged the tray down on the table. "Listen, I'm following the doctor's orders and doing the best I can. Whatever I do for her is wrong. She and I just don't get along as well as she does with you and Willem. We never will!"

I swallowed some lettuce and wiped my mouth. "Maybe if you guys talked about stuff more . . ."

"It's not that easy for us, Louise. You get to see her now, when she's sober and fairly reasonable. She and I have a very rocky history, and neither of us wants to walk back over the rocks. It hurts."

I noticed how worn-out she looked. I got up and gave my mom a squeeze. "Nurse Simon says you're doing a really good job, and that grandmother is lucky to have you."

She tried to smile and she blew her nose. "Thanks. I'm just trying to take care of her every day. I don't have time to rehash the past." She picked up the tray. "Now, if I can get a little vitamin A into her today, I'll feel successful." She half smiled at me. "Be a good girl at Blaise's."

I nodded. Like I really had a choice in the matter.

I knocked on the door of Paradise. Patrice, Blaise's eight-year-old sister, answered the door. "Blaisey, your teacher is here!" she screamed.

I waited, full of angst, in the foyer. Angst was a nice, compact word for anxiety and apprehension.

Blaise came bounding down the stairs. He grinned and grabbed the books from my arms. "Hey, let's go out on the porch, I want to talk to you."

My heart soared. Maybe we were finally going to do something more exciting than word problems.

Blaise jumped into the hammock and gestured at me to sit in a lounge chair.

I watched him sway gently and wished he had suggested we share the hammock.

"So, Louise, the test is in one more week. What do you think my chances are?"

"Excellent. I'm sure you'll pass. You might not get an A, but you'll definitely pass." I smiled. I felt good about that part. I had helped him, and I knew it.

He crossed his arms behind his head and grinned at me. "You are really a nice girl, you know that?"

I blushed.

"No, I mean it. I can't believe how great you've been. So, it's hard to ask you this . . ."

"Ask me what?"

"Could you keep an eye on Patrice for a couple hours for me? Mom went shopping and I'm supposed to watch her, but they called an extra football practice, and I really oughta go."

I was so relieved. For a minute there I thought he was going to ask me to stop coming around. "Oh, sure, Blaise, I'd be glad to."

He jumped up and bolted toward the door. "Thanks, again, you sweet thing!" he called. I heard the door slam.

I shook my head. That was quick. I shrugged and looked out at the pool. I watched a beach ball float and bob—just like my thoughts.

Anne and Becky and my grandmother were always asking me if Blaise had kissed me, or if Blaise had taken me anywhere yet. It bugged me. I always wished I had a more exciting answer. I sighed. Oh well, we did have work to do, and as soon as the test was over, I hoped things would get very romantic. Maybe he was just waiting. Sometimes when we were working on a math problem he would stare at me or touch my hand longer than he needed to. I clung to those memories and went to check on Patrice.

She was playing Barbie in her room.

"Hey, Patrice, I'm going to baby-sit you, okay?"

"I'm too old to be baby-sitted, but you can play Barbie with me if you want." She handed me a Ken and we played wedding. I pretended it was Blaise and me.

Patrice put her Barbie away and closed the big, pink house. "I want to go in our pool, Louise. But I can't unless you come out and watch me. Will you?"

"Sure, let's go."

I watched her swim and dive and do handstands about a million times. She got out and, dripping, walked over to me. "I like you. You're better than Blaisey's other girlfriend."

101

I felt my chest tighten. I shielded my eyes and looked at her. "You mean his old girlfriend, right?"

She wrung her hair out and watched the water fall on my feet. "No, I mean snooty, booby old Debby. She never plays Barbie with me and she's only nice to me if Mommy or Daddy is there, or if Blaise is watching her. The rest of the time she's all creepy. But you're not."

I tried to control my voice. "No, I'm not creepy. I'm nice. I'm so nice that I'm almost invisible. And I bet I'll be real easy to erase."

"Huh?"

"Never mind, Patrice. Are you positive that Debby is still his girlfriend? I mean, maybe it was a long time ago, and you just remembered it now."

Patrice put her hands on her hips. "I'm not stooopid. She was over here last night for Blaisey's birthday. I mean, duh." She went to the edge of the pool. "Watch me again, okay?"

"Okay," I croaked.

When Blaise returned I was waiting for him. Maybe he had used me and was going to dump me, but I would make sure he remembered me. I had a speech all planned to fling in his face. I was going to tell him what a selfish pig he was. I was going to tell him that he and Debby deserved each other. I was going to tell him he was no great loss. Losing my grandmother would be a great loss, losing him would be a pleasure.

But that's not what happened. What happened was that Blaise kissed me.

When Blaise got home, he found me out by the pool. Patrice was inside watching TV. He walked over and sat down next to me. "How'd it go?"

"Fine."

"Look, I got a school jacket today. When I earn a football letter, I'll have Mom sew it on here. And I'll have you to thank for it." He threw the jacket around my shoulders and slid his hand behind my neck. He tilted his head and smiled. "Prepare to be kissed," he whispered.

But nothing could have prepared me for that.

When I could breathe again, I stood up. "You know what, Blaise? That would have meant so much to me yesterday. But today, I know that you're just using me. You've been using me all along." I yanked his jacket from my shoulders and flung it into the pool.

"What is wrong with you?" he yelled. "There's leather on the back of that, it'll be ruined!" He tore off his shoes and dove into the water. He dragged himself out like a wet dog and stood dripping before me.

"Just consider that my final gesture," I said. I turned away and started to cry. "Good luck with your test," I called.

I walked away from Paradise.

Try to erase that!

103

C H A P T E R

12

I heard lots of "I told you so's" for the next week. All except from Willem.

"Things will get better, Louise," he said. "Dey always do." Then he wrapped me up in a big bear hug.

I hung on and tried hard to believe him.

Anne and Becky were nice after they were done gloating.

"Bryan has asked me to the movies this weekend, Louise. He said he knows a real nice guy who would love to go with you."

"No thanks, Beck. I think I'll give up boys for a while and concentrate on school." I knew I also had to concentrate on how to face Blaise at the high school. But I was not going to let him drive me away from skipping a grade!

Anne squeezed my hand and congratulated me for drowning Blaise's jacket. "Good show, Louise!" she exclaimed.

My grandmother was getting quieter and thinner every day. But she recommended some good romance novels for me to read. I finished *Jane Eyre,* and was now on my way to the library for *Pride and Prejudice.*

The last person I expected to see at the library was Debby Stafford. But there she was. Big and full of life.

I parked my bike and tried to step past her. She moved into my path.

"What are you doing here?" I asked. "Waiting for story time?"

She sneered. "Har har. No. I'm waiting for my boyfriend."

I did *not* want to see Blaise. I started to pull my bike back out of the rack, but she put her hand on my arm.

"What's your hurry? You just got here. Not scared of me, are you?" She chomped a wad of gum and blew a pink bubble.

I shook my head and tried to think of a way to avoid seeing the two of them together.

She picked up her hair and wound it around on top of her head. "Don't you want to meet my hunk? He's in there getting a book on how to repair motorcycles. We're gonna be bikers. Dave knows cool."

"Dave?"

"Yeah, you didn't think I'd be boyfriendless for longer than two seconds, did you?" She blew and popped her gum.

"But I thought you were going with Blaise. Weren't you at his birthday the other night?"

"Well, yeah, so? Our parents have been friends since the beginning of time. We always go to each other's family birthdays. We have since we were little brats." She turned her slow wit in my direction. "How come you're askin' me? He's your little jock of a jerk now, isn't he?"

I yanked the bike out and jumped on. I peddled as fast as I could. I had an apology to deliver.

I found Blaise at the pool. I told him I needed to talk to him and he asked me to wait until his break. He was very cool. After all, I had drowned his jacket in cold blood. I paced and sweated and practiced an apology. He came over and sat down. The silence between us was long and heavy. I looked at his familiar profile: I had been staring at it for half the summer, while he studied. I loved the way his hair curled under his ear.

I fought the urge to reach out and touch his hair. "Listen, first of all, I have to apologize for killing your jacket. I want to buy you a new one." I smiled weakly and looked at him.

He shook his head. "No, thanks. I already replaced it."

"Have you already replaced me?" I asked.

He heaved a sigh. "Well, no, Louise. I'm still tryin' to figure out what made you go berserk."

I went back to the beginning and explained.

"So, you see, after Anne saw you guys, I was already suspicious. What Patrice said just pushed me right over the edge. I'm sorry, Blaise. It's hard not to believe what everyone says is true.''

He shook his head. ''Listen, I know what people say about me. None of it's true, but what am I supposed to do? Run around and tell everybody that I'm nice?''

''I'm sorry. Really, really sorry,'' I said. ''I should have come right out and asked you, I guess.''

''Yeah, I guess. Especially before you committed jacket murder.'' He grinned and pulled me close to him. His skin was warm and smelled like suntan lotion.

''So, why were you and Debby at the duck pond?''

He laughed. ''Oh, such trust.''

''Well?''

''Okay, listen, this is just between us, okay?''

I nodded.

''She asked me to meet her there. Her dad lost his job, and their family might have to move. I felt bad for her. Earlier in the year her folks were talking about getting divorced, and I'm the only one she told. I'm the only real friend Debby has. We've known each other since before kindergarten. I guess she feels like she can tell me family stuff. And I feel like I owe her; we did date for quite a while, you know.''

I looked up at him. ''Why did you date her for so long?''

He shrugged. ''I dunno, really. My parents kind of pushed it. They think she's great. And all the other guys thought it was cool that I was with her. But it got boring. All we did was hang out and look good together.''

''Is that all?''

He grinned. ''I won't lie to you, Louise. We kissed and stuff, but it didn't mean much.''

I swallowed. ''Oh.''

''I wanted to get to know you before I kissed you.'' He smiled and I blushed.

''My mama didn't raise a real smart boy, but she raised a real careful one.''

I touched his arm. ''She raised a real nice one. I always thought you were a very nice guy.''

''I'm also a guy who can learn when he has the right teacher,'' he said.

I squealed. ''You passed, didn't you?''

He nodded. ''Yep. Yesterday. And I also got my driver's license. So, how about if we go out on a non-study date tonight?''

I hugged my knees to my chest. ''I would love to go out with you, Blaise Paradise.''

I practically ran over Nurse Simon with my bike. ''Whoa, Louise. Where's your bike helmet?'' she asked.

''I hate those, they wreck your hair,'' I said.

''I know, I know, but they save your head. You really should wear one.'' She dug in her purse for her car keys.

''How's my grandmother? Is she getting any better?''

''Mary Lou isn't doing so great today, I'm afraid. We think the cancer has spread to her spine.'' She stroked my arm and shook her head. "I know these declines are hard to take. How are you coping, dear?"

I chewed the inside of my cheek to keep from crying. It didn't work. "Okay, I guess. At first, I didn't want her to come, and now I don't want her to go." I wiped my nose on my sleeve.

She handed me a tissue from her purse. "Just remember that you are all giving her the best gift you could give."

I nodded. "How's Evan, Mrs. Simon? I heard he was away at scout camp."

"Evan's fine. He's working on his Eagle Scout requirements this summer." She smiled at me. "He used to have quite a crush on you. Did you know that?"

I blushed and nodded. "Yes, I guess I knew. He's a nice boy . . ."

"Just not your type, huh?"

"I guess not."

"Oh, well. You know, he told me once that kids at school only pay attention to him when they make fun of him. He said you didn't do that."

"People can be so mean sometimes."

"And sometimes they can be so good. Who knows why."

"Not me." I waved as she drove away.

I found Mom with my grandmother. She motioned me to sit down. The room was dark.

"How is she?" I whispered.

109

Mom shook her head. "They think the cancer may have spread."

"I know. I talked to Mrs. Simon."

"The doctor said that hearing is the last sense to leave. We should keep talking to her as if she can hear us, because she probably can, even though she can't respond much."

"That's right. So don't sit there and talk about me like I'm gone." My grandmother's hoarse voice rose from her bed.

Mom gasped. "Mom, you scared me. I thought you were asleep."

"Nope. Just dozing. I could use some cool water, Meg."

Mom jumped up. "I'll be right back."

I leaned in. "Frank Sinatra called for you. He says to get back in line and take a number; the line is real short now."

She laughed. She laughed until tears came. "That's a good one, namesake. You're a chip off this old, crumbling block."

"I hope so," I said.

Mom came in with the water. "How come you two always laugh when I'm not here?"

"To annoy you," said her mother.

Mom shrugged. "I give up. You two are on some weird wavelength that I don't receive."

Mary Lou patted her hand. "Don't worry about it, Meg. You're a good girl. Always have been."

Mom beamed. "Thanks, Mom."

The phone rang. Mom went to get it.

"I'm glad you told her that," I said.

"Well, it was Dutch's suggestion. I assumed she knew I thought that. She knows I love her."

"I don't think people know that, if you don't say it," I said.

"Well, in my day, we did not sit around and talk about our feelings. You went to work, put food on the table, and hoped not to die of polio or diphtheria or some other horror." She tried to lift her glass, but her hand shook. I held it for her.

"You did the best you could, just like Mom, I guess."

She nodded.

Mom came in. "It's for you, Louise. It's Blaise."

I jumped up. "Oh, my gosh! I forgot to tell you guys. It was all a big misunderstanding. He wasn't really seeing Debby. And he's asked me to go out tonight. But, I don't know. Maybe I should stay here and visit."

"Don't you dare," said my grandmother. "Don't start this death vigil stuff. I have told you and Simon and Dutch that I am hanging on for the changing of the leaves. I mean it."

I looked at Mom. She nodded. "Go have fun."

I ran to the phone.

"I'm sorry it took so long," I said.

"Geez. I thought you were standing me up on the phone!"

"No. My grandmother isn't doing too well today. I thought maybe I should stay home with her."

"Oh, yeah, I remember. You told me a little about it when we were studying. I'm sorry, Louise. It's okay with me if you need to be home."

"No, really. I asked and they said I should go. I think it's okay. I think my grandma just might fool all of them and hang on until the fall. She says she wants to see the leaves change."

"Hey, that gives me an idea."

"What?"

"Are you in the mood for a little adventure tonight?"

I paused. But not for long. "Blaise, I'm ready for anything."

"Great. I'll pick you up in an hour."

C H A P T E R
13

The doorbell rang and I charged to open the door. Blaise stood there, smiling and holding a corsage. ''To make up for the one I forgot,'' he said.

I laughed and pulled him into the room. He pinned the flower to my T-shirt. Then he tipped my chin upward with his finger and brushed his lips against mine. I was surprised at how soft his mouth was. Somehow I always imagined that boys' mouths would be rough. I was wrong.

''Thanks for remembering,'' I said.

''Better late than never.''

''Where are we going, anyway? My curiosity is piqued.'' I held his hand shyly.

''You'll see,'' he said with a grin.

''Okay, okay. I'll be surprised. Listen, my grandmother wants to see you again before we leave. Do you mind?''

"No. I want to see her, so I can show her that I know your name now."

I smiled. "You're forgiven for that."

"Hey, I was really nervous that night. I thought you would think I was just some dumb jock. I was afraid you'd talk about stuff I didn't know about."

"Well, you didn't seem nervous to me." I squeezed his hand.

He squeezed back.

My grandmother was sitting up in bed, talking to Willem, who stood up when we came in. He extended his hand to Blaise. "Hello, Blaise. How are things with you?"

"Fine, sir."

"You remember Blaise, don't you, grandmother?" I asked.

"Of course. I never forget a hunk." She smiled. "I see you have been to the florist, my boy. I approve."

Blaise grinned. "I'm trying to make a good impression on you, ma'am. Louise always says how much she admires you."

"Oh, she does, does she? Well, it's mutual. I'm afraid she has charmed this old snake charmer." She turned away and began to cough. Willem jumped up and held her head over a bucket we kept by the bed.

I took Blaise out in the hallway. "She's been getting a lot worse the past few days," I said.

He held my hands. "You're shaking, Louise."

"I know. I'm scared."

114

"Maybe we should just stay here," he offered.

"No, I think I'd like to get out for a little while. I'm sure she'll make it until the fall. I really am." I looked back in the room and made a silent bargain: *Please let her live until autumn. I'll be good forever, if you just let her have that one thing.*

The hacking from inside the room stopped.

"Let's go," I said.

We got in the car and headed out of town. Blaise pulled into a hamburger joint and ordered at the drive-up window.

"Okay, Blaise. Where are we going, and why are we eating on the run, like two escaped criminals?"

He drove and bit into his burger. "Because I think we should elope."

"What?"

He laughed. "Chill out. I'm kidding. I heard that the leaves have begun to change up at Mountain Lake. The elevation is so much higher, that the leaves go first up there. They won't be really bright yet, but they will be colored." He glanced at my smiling face. "I thought, for your grandma, it would be . . ."

I touched his arm. "Thanks a lot."

He shrugged. "It's okay."

We drove in comfortable silence until the massive stone hotel came into view. I sighed. "I just can't get over how pretty this place is."

"I can't get over how pretty you are," he said.

"Oh, come on. I'm smart but I'm not pretty, Blaise. I know that."

"Louise, you don't know as much as you think about some things. I've dated girls that everyone said were beautiful. Everyone was wrong." He pulled the car around the last bend and we parked. I decided to let him have the last word.

"Let's head up Bear Cliffs Trail. It makes a circle, so we'll end up back down here." He grabbed my hand and we headed up into the leaves.

We pulled up to my house and looked at the blazing porch lights. "My stepdad is on duty," I said.

"Yeah, he's a good guy. Listen, Louise, I gotta get home. It's getting late. Tell your grandma I said I hope she likes the leaves, okay?"

I nodded. "This was the nicest thing, Blaise. I'm so happy that we found so many colored leaves already. I'll put them up around her room, while she waits for the fall colors." I gathered the leaves in my arms. "Thanks again. I'll see you soon, okay?"

He nodded. "You'll see me all the time."

I waved until he turned off our street. I ran inside, trailing leaves.

Willem stopped me in the foyer. "Your grandmudder is not doing well."

"What?" I whispered.

"We think it is a coma."

I dropped the leaves around our feet. "Oh no! Not

while I was gone. We went to get leaves for her to see . . ."

Willem put his arms around me and spoke quietly. "Try to be calm. It will be better for you if you can accept what it is that happens." He stooped down to gather the leaves. "You go in with your family. The leaves I will bring in a short time."

I stood there.

"Go ahead, Louise."

I went to her room. Mom was sitting by the bed. She looked up and reached her arms out to me. I sat on the edge of the chair and we cried.

Mom wiped her eyes. "The doctor said she could be like this for hours, days, or weeks. They never know."

"Maybe she can still come out of it," I said.

Mom shrugged. "She can still hear us, dear. Remember? Sometimes she responds to something I say. Sometimes she speaks. Just a little while ago she said her mother was here, standing at the foot of the bed."

Tingles went up my spine. "Maybe her mother came to help her die."

"I wish I knew," said Mom. She stood up and stretched. "I'm going to get a cup of coffee. Call me if anything changes."

I nodded. Willem came in and put the leaves around the room. "Look at dis. Louise and her friend brought you the leaves of fall. I am putting them up in your room for you to see and smell." He placed some on her bedcovers. He picked up her hand and ran her fingers over the veins of the leaf. Her fingers moved.

"She knows we are here, I am sure of dat." He kissed her forehead. "I'm going to get a fresh wet cloth."

My chin quivered and I shook all over. I was afraid to touch her. I leaned forward and gently touched her hand. She felt cool. "Hey, it's me." I said. "I found you some leaves while we wait for the fall. I know you'll be here in October. I just know it. You're going to prove all of them wrong." I stroked her arm and put my mouth right next to her face. "I know you can make it, Grandmother." I wiped the tears off my face and chin. "So, I'll see you tomorrow. Tot straks!"

Her lips moved, and I put my ear to her mouth so I could hear her.

"*Tot ziens,* namesake," she said finally.

C H A P T E R
14

Grandmother hung on until morning, then she left with her mother. At least, that's what I hope happened. Nurse Simon helped make the funeral arrangements.

Mrs. Simon came into the kitchen and patted my back. "Your grandmother was a very special person," she said.

"I think so, too," I said. I wrung a well-used tissue in my hand and thought that she was definitely not sketched in pencil. I wiped my eyes for the millionth time that morning. "I was sure she'd make it until fall. I really felt that. It was all she asked for in all the time she's been here. I felt like I made a deal and someone broke their promise." My shoulders shook and my chest heaved. I couldn't control myself.

"I know how you feel, dear. But you have to understand. Some things happen when they must. Like death—and the changing of the leaves."

* * *

Grandmother had asked to be cremated, so we honored her wish. We kept the ashes at home. Mom said we would wait until the colors were blazing, then we would hike up into the mountains and scatter grandmother's ashes amidst the veil of leaves. "I think the colors will be a natural, vibrant tribute to her. She deserves that much on her final journey," Mom told us.

Three days after her death, Mom and I were cleaning out her room. "She wanted you to have her book of poetry, Louise." Mom handed me the book and smiled. "I know that meant a lot to her. It's all she had of her own mother."

I held the worn-leather binding and rifled through the pages. "Look, there's a bookmark here." I read the poem on that page and started to cry. I handed the book to my mom.

"This is her final gesture to you, Louise." She cleared her throat and read the anonymous poem aloud.

> Do not stand at my grave and weep,
> I am not there, I do not sleep.
> I am the sunlight of ripened grain,
> I am the gentle autumn's rain.
> When you awaken in the morning hush,
> I am that swift uplifting rush
> Of quiet birds in circled flight.
> I am the soft stars that shine at night.
> Do not stand at my grave and cry,
> I am not there, I did not die.

Mom closed the book and we cried together. The doorbell rang, and Mom blew her nose and wiped her face on her work shirt.

I followed her to the foyer. It was the UPS man. He carried two boxes inside and Mom signed for them.

"Oh, my gosh, Louise. This is that stuff from Florida that she had in storage all those years. Remember that junk she insisted I have sent here? She said she didn't even remember what was in them."

I helped her drag them into the living room. I watched as she slit them open. "It took long enough for that guy to send them here. I mean, maybe there was stuff in here she wanted," I said.

Mom gasped and sat back on her heels.

"What's in it, Mom?" I jumped up and went over to the boxes.

She held up report cards, a child's drawings, and awards. "Me. I'm in these boxes." She looked at me and smiled through her tears. "I thought she lost all this stuff. I thought she threw it away."

I picked up a drawing of a little girl holding her mother's hand. "Did you draw this?"

She nodded and ran her fingers over the old, faded markings. "I drew it in Mrs. Webb's second-grade class. I guess I understood something then that I forgot as I got older." She stared at the childish images. "Her hand was always there for me. It might have been unsteady, but it was always there."

And then I heard it—just as clear as if she were next to me. My grandmother's voice said, *"Tot straks, namesake. Tot straks."*

And I think she was laughing.